FORGIVENESS FOUND IN HONEY GROVE

A BRAXTON FAMILY ROMANCE BOOK 4

ANNE-MARIE MEYER

To my family

SHE'S AN IRS AUDITOR DESPERATE TO PROVE HERSELF.

HE'S A COWBOY TRYING TO HOLD ONTO HIS RANCH.

LOVE WAS NOT ON THE AGENDA.

ONE

JACKSON

JACKSON LIFTED the scotch to his lips and took a sip, hoping to calm the jumble of nerves that had cemented themselves in his stomach. He wasn't normally a drinker, but this trip had him running to anything that would calm him down.

He was going back to Honey Grove. Back to his hometown. Where Isabel Andrews was.

Was he crazy?

The plane dipped, causing his stomach to become airborne. He clutched the armrests of his seat as Brooklyn, the flight attendant, appeared from the tiny kitchen in the back.

"Sorry, Mr. Braxton. Barry said there might be some turbulence."

Jackson shot her a smile as he tried to force down his anxiety.

He was a successful businessman. He had accomplished everything that he'd left Honey Grove in search of. He was going back for his brother Jonathan's wedding, and that was it. There was no need to feel so out of sorts about seeing Isabel.

Besides, she'd moved on. She was engaged, and he was... well, he was happy.

He worked on his smile a few more times, trying to figure out which one sent the right message. He was happy. He was happy. He was happy.

His cheeks grew tired, so he dropped his lips to a frown, grabbed his glass of scotch, and took another sip. He set the glass down with a sigh. The alcohol was not making him feel better, and his mom, Sondra, would smell it on him if he consumed much more.

That woman was a bloodhound about alcohol—and about potential marriage material for her children.

"Are you finished?" Brooklyn asked as she appeared next to him. "Do you want me to get you another?"

Jackson shook his head as he handed the glass back to her. "I'm okay. Thank you though." Then he rubbed his temples as nausea hit him. Drinking on an empty stomach always made him feel sick. "Maybe some cookies? I need to eat." In his haste to leave this morning, he'd forgotten breakfast.

Brooklyn nodded. "Of course. I'll get something whipped up for you."

Jackson shot her a smile, and she disappeared into the kitchen.

Now alone, Jackson leaned his head back and took in a deep breath. He closed his eyes and concentrated on his breathing. He could do this. He could handle returning to Honey Grove.

He could even handle seeing Isabel.

The nausea hit him harder as her sandy blonde hair and wide smile filled his mind. It had been years since he'd seen her. Touched her. Kissed her.

Why was her memory so vivid? It was like he could reach out and feel her next to him.

Clearing his throat, he opened his eyes. This was getting him nowhere. He needed to focus on something else.

He leaned over his chair and pulled out his laptop. Messages and email notifications chimed as he dove into work.

He'd been doing that a lot lately. Focusing on work. When he lost himself in his responsibilities, he could make every gaping hole in his heart disappear. He scoffed. That was a lie even he wasn't believing anymore.

But, eventually, he lost himself so completely in answering emails and working on his big accounts that he didn't notice Brooklyn standing next to him with a plate of filet mignon and mashed potatoes.

"You're a life saver," he said as he adjusted his laptop so she could set the plate down next to him. His stomach growled.

She laughed and handed him a set of utensils. Then she left him to eat in silence.

One plate of food and an hour later, Barry announced over the intercom that they were making their final descent.

Brooklyn came to collect his dishes, and Jackson returned his computer to his bag and sat back. It was amazing how the distraction of work and food helped clear his mind.

Even though the thought of seeing Isabel still nipped at the back of his mind, he was more content. The reason why he left Honey Grove made its way back into his mind and helped ground him.

Isabel wasn't the one for him, and he wasn't meant for her.

Her dad had made that pretty clear the night Jackson had planned to ask her to marry him.

Jackson Braxton was never going to be good enough for Mr. Andrews' daughter. He hadn't minced words about it. No, poor, rowdy, eighteen-year-old was going to drag Isabel down with him. Period.

So Jackson disappeared to New York, licking his wounds. Determined to prove Dirk Andrews wrong.

And now, with multiple zeros in his bank account, Jackson had become the man he'd wanted to be. He'd accomplished everything that Mr. Andrews had claimed he would never achieve. He'd negated every reason Mr. Andrews had given for Jackson to walk away from Isabel.

So why was he so nervous about coming home? He had nothing to be embarrassed about.

The plane lurched as the wheels touched down, throwing Jackson forward. He gripped the armrests and took a few deep breaths.

He could do this. He was determined to do this.

The plane taxied into the hangar, and a few minutes later, Jackson grabbed his suitcase and headed toward the exit. He smiled at Brooklyn, who blushed as he walked past.

He felt her hand rest on his arm. "Hey," she whispered, like she wasn't sure about what she was doing.

Jackson paused and glanced down at her. He quirked an eyebrow as he studied her deep brown eyes and fair, freckled skin. "Yeah?" he asked.

She blinked a few times, and her blush deepened. "I live in Jordan. If you get bored and want to do something, call me." She pressed a piece of paper into the palm of his hand.

Jackson's gaze flicked down and then back up to her. Was she hitting on him? The earnest look in her eyes made him smile.

It wasn't like this was a surprise to him, but it did feel a tad strange. Especially since he'd spent basically the whole trip obsessing about Isabel.

But Brooklyn looked so earnest as she peered up at him that he didn't want to disappoint her. So he leaned toward her and smiled. "Thanks for the offer," he said as he slipped her number into his pocket.

She giggled and nodded.

"Enjoy the flight?" Barry boomed as he emerged from the cockpit. His gaze swept over Jackson and Brooklyn, his bushy eyebrows rising. "Am I interrupting?"

Jackson shook his head as he turned toward the pilot. "Nope. The flight was amazing."

Barry let out a laugh and slapped Jackson on the back. "Enjoy going home."

Great. Just when Jackson thought he had a handle on his feelings, Barry had to bring it up. "I will," Jackson said under his breath.

Once he was off the plane, he blew out his breath as his thoughts returned to Brooklyn and her number in his pocket. Sure, he really wasn't in the right place, headspace-wise, to start a relationship, but she was cute. And maybe she was the kind of distraction he needed.

Odds were good that being around his family was going to be overwhelming. Having an escape plan seemed wise.

After walking through the hangar, he climbed into the car that had been waiting for him. He glanced down at his watch. Fifteen minutes until Jenna's plane landed.

He told the driver to head to the passenger pickup area and leaned back, resting his head on the seat behind him. He closed his eyes and forced his mind to clear.

It wasn't long before Jenna rapped on the window and then pulled the door open and climbed in. She smiled. "Jacky!" she exclaimed as she reached over and wrapped her arms around him.

Jackson laughed as he hugged his sister. They'd been

inseparable since they were kids. And if he were honest with himself, he missed her. A lot.

"Jenna Pee Pants," he said.

She groaned as she pulled back. "Can we just let that name die?"

Jackson shook his head as he handed the driver the address of their parents' house in Honey Grove. "Yeah, I don't think so. It's just...so good."

Jenna reached out and punched his arm. Jackson feigned pain as he clutched his arm but then shot her a smile. "Nice try. Still the weakling, I see."

"Bite me." Jenna tried to glare at him then busted up laughing. "Man, I missed you," she said, her voice growing quiet.

Jackson studied his sister. Her normally goofy disposition was gone. He could see stress lines etched into her skin. "Porter's an idiot," he said.

Jenna closed her eyes and nodded. He could see that she was trying to be strong, but it was taking a lot of work.

"Yeah, he is." She took a few deep breaths, and then her familiar smile emerged as she opened her eyes. "But we aren't going to talk about him ever again. Deal?" She reached into her purse and grabbed a bag of M&M's. She tipped the opening toward him. Jackson nodded, and she poured a couple into his hand. "Let's talk about Isabel and what you are going to do if you see her."

Jackson groaned. Leave it to his sister to want to be part

of his business. "Jenna. No talking about Porter. No talking about Isabel."

Jenna raised her eyebrows and then let out a sigh. "Fine." Her phone chimed as she shoved a few M&M's into her mouth. She dug around in her purse and emerged triumphant with her phone in hand. After a few seconds, she glanced over at him. "You gotta take me to Layla's shop. Apparently, I need to be fitted for my dress."

Jackson groaned. That sounded like the last thing he wanted to do. "I'll let you take the car. Just drop me off at home first."

Jenna leaned in. "You really want to face Mom alone?"

Jackson hesitated as thoughts of Sondra Braxton following after him, asking him when he was going to get married, floated through his mind. He turned and narrowed his eyes at Jenna. "Good point." Then he let out his breath in a slow burst. "Just a few minutes, right? Then you'll go home with me?"

Jenna giggled as she downed a few more pieces of candy. She held up her hand like she was being sworn in at court. "I promise."

Jackson leaned forward and gave the driver the new address.

Once Jackson settled back in his seat, Jenna started telling him about her apartment and how grateful she was to get out of Seattle She was ready to leave that city and all her memories of Porter in the dust. Jackson hadn't always been protective of his little sister, but once she'd been old enough to date, those feelings wouldn't leave him alone.

She had rapidly gone from his annoying sister to his best friend.

Fifteen minutes later, the car stopped in front of one of the long buildings in downtown Honey Grove. The corner shop sported the words *Braxton Dresses*. Jackson smiled as he shook his head.

He was pretty sure his mom died when James and Layla had picked that name. It was one of her dreams, to see the Braxton name up in lights. Add in Jonathan's status as an NFL player, and Mom was in heaven.

"Holy wow," Jenna said as she stared out the car window. "Mom must have freaked."

Jackson laughed. Sondra wasn't a mysterious person—everyone in the family had her pegged. Jackson grabbed the door handle and stepped out. "Come on. Let's get this over with."

Going to a dress fitting wasn't the most exciting thing for him, but it beat sitting at home and being berated by his mom. And it definitely was a distraction from his thoughts.

But, as he stepped out onto the sidewalk, he glanced around at the people walking by, and his stomach tightened. That was the curse of returning to the place where the girl you once loved still lived. He couldn't help being on edge, wondering when he was going to see her next.

Did she know he was coming home? Was she as nervous as he was?

He was working his body into knots again, so Jackson forced his thoughts to calm as he made his way around to where Jenna was waiting for him.

She took in a deep breath as she glanced over at him. "Ready?"

Jackson nodded, and they walked side by side into the small shop. Lighthearted laughter carried from the back, perking up Jackson's ears.

He paused as the shop door shut behind him. He recognized that laugh. His heart twisted as Isabel appeared from the back room. She was walking in front of a very pregnant woman who Jackson could only assume was Layla.

After a quick marriage a few months ago, she and James had moved to Honey Grove. James took over running the family business, Braxton Construction, and Layla opened a wedding shop. James hadn't asked anyone to fly down for the wedding. He said all he cared about was marrying the woman of his dreams.

That thought paused in Jackson's mind as his gaze landed on Isabel. Everything about her was so familiar. The curvature of her features. The way her blonde hair danced around her shoulders. Her lips... Every memory of her came rushing back, slamming into his heart and taking his breath away.

"Jackson," she said as her gaze landed on his face. She looked as startled as he felt.

"Isabel," Jenna said, stepping forward and pulling Isabel

into an awkward hug. She turned Isabel so she could raise her eyebrows at Jackson.

He'd never been more grateful for his sister. He needed a minute to compose himself.

"Jenna?" Isabel asked, surprised. "It's good to see you."

Jenna pulled back. "You too. What are you doing here?"

Jackson pushed his hands through his hair as he watched Isabel hold up a dress that was draped over her arm. "Picking up my dress."

Jenna let out a forced laugh. "That's right. I heard you're tying the knot." Her gaze flicked back to Jackson and then returned to Isabel. "Who's the lucky guy?"

Jackson could see Isabel's shoulders tighten. He wondered if it had to do with her fiancé or the fact that he was there, listening to their conversation.

"Just an investor who moved into town. He's...great."

Jackson's ears perked. He knew Isabel. He knew her mannerisms. He could pick out the inflection in her voice. She was lying.

"That's great. When's the day?"

Isabel tipped her head to the side as if she were checking to see if Jackson was still listening. Jackson dropped his gaze to the floor. "Two Saturdays from now," she replied.

"Well, we're just here for Jonathan's wedding this weekend, and then we're gone." Jenna clapped her hands and turned to Layla. "I have a dress I'm supposed to be fitted for?"

Layla was standing off to the side, watching the interaction. When Jenna approached, Layla gave her a wide smile. "Of course." They embraced. "It's so good to finally meet you."

Jenna kept her arm around Layla's shoulders as she nodded toward Jackson. "Come on, I need your help."

Grateful for the excuse, Jackson moved to follow his sister. Just as he passed by Isabel, her soft voice stopped him.

"It's good to see you again," she said.

Jackson fought the urge to turn and look at her. If he did, his heart would break more than it already was. But he couldn't just ignore her. So, he nodded and said, "You too." Then he headed after Layla and Jenna.

He wasn't sure what Isabel did after he left, but he did know one thing—he was right to be nervous about coming home.

It was going to be a lot harder than he'd thought.

TWO

ISABEL

ISABEL HUGGED her dress to her chest as she pushed out of Layla's shop. Her gaze was fixed on the ground, and she had never wanted to get out of a place so fast.

Seeing Jackson like that was the last thing she'd needed. Especially when it already felt like her life was crumbling down around her.

Desperate to get to her car before the tears started, Isabel quickened her pace. By the time she reached the driver's door, a tear had escaped and rolled down her cheek.

Her life was a mess.

Pulling hard on the door handle, she slipped into the seat, dumped her dress next to her, and slammed the door closed. She sat there for a moment with both hands on the steering wheel as the hot, sticky car air settled in around her.

Not wanting to be a crying *and* sweating mess, Isabel

shoved her keys into the ignition. Her car sputtered a few times but didn't turn over.

Crap.

She tried it again.

Nothing.

Frustration and embarrassment coursed through her. Really? Today of all days her car wasn't going to start.

Just her luck. Her first interaction with Jackson was topped off with her car breaking down.

Cursing under her breath, she tightened her grip on the wheel and stared down at her lap. This was not how she'd seen her life going.

When Jackson left her in the lurch, she swore she would make something of herself. And yet, here she sat years later with nothing but mounding debt and a broken life to show for it.

If Jackson knew, he would laugh.

He'd broken her heart once, and she doubted he had enough humanity in him to not do it again.

Just as she thought the words, regret filled her chest. She knew that wasn't true. Jackson had been one of the sweetest, most loving guys she'd ever met. But he'd left. Without a word. Without an explanation.

Gone.

Tears welled up in her eyes, and she had to shush her mind before the waterworks started.

Determined to get out of there before the Braxtons came back out of the bridal store, she swung open her door and stepped out. She pulled the release to the hood and walked around to open it.

She stared in at the engine, completely lost. It was comical that she was attempting to look like she knew what she was doing. Dad had always helped her with all the mechanical stuff.

Tears welled up again.

Not anymore. Not since he was diagnosed with Alzheimer's. Now, he barely knew who she was. Which she wasn't complaining about. It just made her sad that she was alone. Bobby, her fiancé, was gone on yet another business trip, leaving her to plan their wedding while working full time in the hope of getting her life together so that Dad could finally come home.

Six months ago, he fell and broke his hip. Things never really healed correctly, so he was forced to use a wheelchair. Add the need for round-the-clock care for his memory, and she was in a pickle. She had no money to remodel the house so that her dad could get around, so he was stuck in a nursing home. A place she'd sworn she would never let him end up.

It had also thrown her engagement into disarray. They couldn't come to an agreement on what to do with her dad. Bobby wanted him to stay in the nursing home so they could start their life together, but Isabel couldn't turn her back on the only man who'd never left her.

Frustrated, Isabel reached into the engine and fiddled around with some hoses. Just as she grabbed one, its coupling slipped, and she was sprayed with some dark, murky liquid.

She screamed and jumped back, slamming her head into the hood. She winced and rubbed the bump that was now forming there.

This was just great.

"Wow. That was...entertaining," Jackson's familiar voice said from behind her.

Isabel closed her eyes for a moment as she tipped her face up toward the sky. Seriously? Why did fate hate her?

She swallowed and took in a deep breath. Then, when she felt as ready as she would ever be, she turned and forced a smile.

Of course, Jackson had to look so incredibly good. He had on a light-blue button-up shirt with the sleeves rolled up and dark dress pants. He didn't look like he'd aged a bit. Being an adult looked good on him. Why did he have to look so put together? On top of that, he looked like he dripped money. Even his haircut looked expensive.

Darn him.

His gaze swept over her, making her feel like an even bigger idiot. She was completely covered in what looked like motor oil—or something similar.

"Car troubles?" he asked as he stepped closer to her. "Can I take a look?"

The breeze picked up and surrounded her with the smell of his cologne. It was a mixture of woods and spice.

And it was familiar, even though Isabel knew he couldn't have afforded that cologne as a teenager.

Isabel stepped back as she watched Jackson dip down to look at her engine. He rested a hand on the outside of the car, and she couldn't help but notice his muscle ripple under the skin of his forearm.

Why did he even wear button-up shirts if he was going to roll up the sleeves? Who was he trying to impress?

Needing to get the heck out of here, she forced all thoughts of Jackson's body from her mind and asked, "So, can you fix it?"

Jackson tipped his face toward her, and, of course, his gaze ran over her body once more. Then he straightened and brushed his hands together. "You should probably call a tow truck. I don't think this car is going anywhere."

Isabel's heart sank. She had work at Humanitarian Hearts this afternoon and then a full shift at the Italian Shoppe this evening. She couldn't be out a car.

"Are you sure?" she asked, not really to him, just to the cosmos that were so excited to dump another crappy situation in her lap.

"Well, since that's supposed to be in there"—Jackson pointed from her oil-splattered shirt to the engine—"I'm guessing you won't get this to go anywhere if it's not attached to a tow truck." He shoved his hands into his front pockets and shrugged. "But I'm no mechanic."

Isabel's eyes felt as if they were going to well up—again. Not wanting to lose her cool in front of Jackson, she nodded and went to grab her phone. She emerged from the car to find Jackson on his phone, talking to someone.

He was a few feet away, speaking in low tones. She wasn't sure who he was talking to, and even though she wanted to listen in, she knew she'd lost the privilege of knowing who he was talking to years ago.

He had moved on and so had she...

Even though right now, as she studied him, her body was saying something completely different. Old feelings that should have been completely dead didn't seem to be as extinct as she'd thought.

Jackson turned and met her gaze, raising his eyebrows. Of course he would catch her staring at him.

Add it to the big stinking pile of bad luck she seemed to be dragging around.

A few seconds later, Jackson hung up. "Zippy's can't come get you for a few hours. Apparently, there's some machinery stuck just off the freeway that he has to deal with first." Jackson slipped his phone into his back pocket. "But they'll get to you when they can."

Isabel stared at him. Had he just set up a tow truck for her? "Um, thanks?" she said, the words coming out more like a question.

Jackson met her gaze and then dropped his eyes, blowing out his breath in a slow stream. He shrugged. "Come on, Izzie. We were friends once. I think we can do that again."

Friends? Really? They'd pretty much planned out their

wedding. All he'd had to do was ask her dad for permission, and she would have run away with him. She'd loved him. And then he'd disappeared without a word.

She swallowed against the emotional lump in her throat and forced a smile. "Of course. Friends."

Ugh, that word tasted bitter on her tongue. Did Jackson feel the same? She peeked over at him to study his reaction. She couldn't really read it—he looked so stoic and relaxed.

Which just made her feel worse.

"Well, thanks," she said as she marched over to the car. She grabbed her purse from the front seat, swung it onto her shoulder, and slammed the door, locking the car as she stepped away.

It was a thirty-minute walk to her house, and she knew she would be a sweaty mess by the time she got there. After taking a shower and having to walk to Humanitarian Hearts, she was going to be late. Might as well call them to let them know.

"Can I give you a ride?" Jackson asked.

Isabel paused, not sure if she heard him right. "I'm sorry, what?" She turned to see Jackson with an uneasy expression on his face.

His shoulders were hunched, and his hands shoved into his pockets. He looked just as startled as she felt. He glanced around and then cleared his throat. "I can give you a ride if you need one. My car service just dropped a car off for me."

She couldn't believe what she was hearing. "Car service?"

He shrugged. "I didn't really want a driver driving me around my hometown."

It was like he was speaking a different language. "Driver?"

"Yeah," Jackson said as if he didn't know what to do with her awkward responses.

She clutched her purse and nodded. "Sure. Thanks." It wasn't like she had anyone else to call. And she really needed some A/C and a minute to catch her breath.

Jackson looked relieved as he pulled out his keys and headed back to the dress shop. "Let me tell Jenna, and I'll be right back." He was gone before Isabel could even respond.

Now alone, she slammed her car hood shut and leaned against it. Her mind was reeling. She was going to voluntarily get into a car with Jackson Braxton. The boy who'd broken her heart.

Was she insane?

Glancing down at her watch, she confirmed her suspicions—it might be insane, but she needed to take him up on his offer if she wanted to get to work on time.

A few minutes later, Jackson returned. He looked a little annoyed, but when his gaze landed on Isabel, he perked up. "Jenna's going to get a ride with Layla," he said as he nodded toward the sidewalk that lead around the building. "Come on, I'm parked over here."

Isabel tightened her grip on her purse strap as she followed him. She wasn't sure how she felt about any of this, and grabbing onto something seemed to ground her. They rounded the corner, and Jackson walked over to a black Lincoln. She tried not to sigh as she realized what she'd suspected all along.

Jackson had made it. He was rich. He probably had the life he'd dreamed about when they were kids. And he'd done it without her.

She swallowed as her heart broke all over again. What was Jackson going to think when he dropped her off at the same old house Isabel had lived in her whole life? Would he judge her?

Probably.

She was stuck in the same old town, in the same old house, living the same old life as when they were together. She hadn't changed.

And she was okay with that. She knew why she'd stayed. Her dad needed her, and she wanted to be there for him. That was never a question for her. But there were moments when she wondered what her life would have been if she'd left. She wondered if she would be happier than she was trying to be right now.

She wondered if she had been more adventurous, would she have been enough? Maybe then Jackson wouldn't have run away like he did.

She swallowed against the lump in her throat.

Jackson pulled open the passenger door and waited for her to climb in. Just like the gentleman Sondra Braxton had taught all her boys to be. Once Isabel was situated, Jackson shut the door and jogged to the driver's side.

He glanced over at her as he slipped his key into the ignition, and the engine roared to life. "Aren't you forgetting something?" he asked, nodding toward her car.

She glanced back. "I don't think so."

He quirked an eyebrow. "Your dress?"

Embarrassment flooded her body and settled in her cheeks. She shook her head. "I'll get it when my car's done. After all, I don't need it today."

Jackson watched her for a moment and then shrugged as he shifted into reverse. "Suit yourself."

THREE

JACKSON

THE SILENCE in the car was deafening. Jackson's mind was flooded with everything he'd wanted to say to Isabel from the moment he left Honey Grove. He'd never been able to gather enough courage to talk to her, though, and now those thoughts, questions, and feelings were rushing through his head and confusing the heck out of him.

Isabel sighed and tipped her face toward the window. She wrapped her arms around her chest, drawing Jackson's focus back over to her.

She was still the perfect girl he remembered. The sun shone through the windshield, highlighting her creamy, white skin.

Out of instinct, he rubbed the pads of his fingers with his thumb. Even though it had been so long since he'd touched her, his receptors hadn't forgotten the feel of her.

He knew what she felt like, smelled like. She had filled his soul. His entire being.

And for the past eight years, he'd convinced himself he didn't care. She was in the past. But it was hard to ignore the past when it was sitting next to him in the front seat.

Isabel was very real, and his senses were letting him know.

He cleared his throat.

"So, when's the big day?" he asked.

Isabel glanced over at him. "In two weeks," she said as she hugged her chest tighter.

Jackson didn't have a lot of experience with people who were about to get married, but he always assumed that they would be happier than Isabel seemed to be.

"Wow." The word hung in the air, all strange and awkward. Desperate to redeem himself, he stumbled to say, "I'm happy for you."

He didn't want her to question what that *wow* meant.

Isabel nodded. "Thanks. I'm happy too."

Jackson gripped the steering wheel tighter. He knew Isabel a lot better than she seemed to be giving him credit for right now. That was not her happy voice. He hated the fact that he knew her smiles, that he knew the tone of her voice like the back of his hand. Something was bothering her.

And it hurt that she wasn't being honest with him.

But he wasn't that guy for her anymore. It wasn't his job

to make her happy. It was her fiancé's job, and he was certainly *not* her fiancé.

Jackson waved toward the road in front of them. "Where to?"

She hesitated before she rattled off the address of her childhood home.

Jackson glanced over at her to see her face tip toward her lap like she was embarrassed. Which was stupid. Why would she be embarrassed about where she lived? It wasn't like he'd never been there.

Before he could stop himself, Jackson asked, "How's your dad?"

It sounded like a simple question, but there was so much meaning behind it. Mr. Andrews. The man who told him he would never bless their marriage. Who told Jackson that he wasn't good enough for his daughter.

Jackson wanted to know how that man was doing.

"He's um...good." Isabel's voice was quiet—another sign that there was something wrong.

Why was she lying like this?

Before he could say anything more, he pulled into her driveway. And maybe that was a good thing. He needed a minute to focus his thoughts before he spoke. Isabel seemed in a hurry to leave the car, and, not wanting to lock her in, he allowed her to open the door and step out.

She murmured a quick, "thanks" and then took off toward the front door.

Jackson sat there, staring after her. The familiar gray

house wasn't what it used to be. The paint was peeling, and the windows foggy. The grass looked as if it needed to be cut —definitely not something Dirk Andrews would have allowed to happen years ago.

It was all so...strange. Isabel wasn't the same person he remembered. Even this house was different. Everything felt off, and Jackson wasn't sure what he thought about any of it.

Before he realized what he was doing, he shut off the engine and pulled open his door. Even though he hadn't seen her for years, he couldn't leave Isabel like this. Something was wrong. And it was something more than just her car breaking down.

He shoved his hands into his front pockets and strode up the walkway. Once he got to the front door, he raised his hand and rapped a few times. He paused, straining to hear sound on the other side.

Was Mr. Andrews home? Where had Isabel gone?

When no answer came, Jackson glanced around and found the same gnome standing guard by the door. Its red paint was chipping, and its nose was worn off. And, if Jackson remembered right, there was a key taped to the bottom.

Reaching down, he picked it up and flipped it over. He cheered inside as he removed the key from the porcelain.

After he pulled the key free, he shoved it into the lock and turned, praying Isabel wouldn't mace him.

He pushed open the door. The house looked as if time had stood still. Everything was just as he remembered it eight years ago. The couches were the same. The placement of the coffee table was the same.

It was clean but old.

"Isabel?" Jackson called, glancing around.

The silence was interrupted only by the ticking of the grandfather clock on the wall. The same one he remembered from when he and Isabel spent nights cuddled up on the couch, watching movies together.

Clearing his throat, he pushed away the memories of her and walked further into the house. He remembered every room, every corner, like the back of his hand.

Once he got to the stairs that were just off the kitchen, he stared at them. Isabel's room was up there, and he was pretty sure that's where she was.

He glanced up and then back down, wondering what the heck he was doing in her house. Was he crazy? Why had he come in here?

He swallowed as embarrassment filled his chest. He ran his hands through his hair and suddenly felt parched. He grabbed a glass and filled it with water.

The sound of footsteps on the stairs made him freeze with his hand on the faucet. Heat coursed through his body as he tried to figure out what he was going to say to Isabel. What reason could he possibly give her for standing in her house, uninvited?

"Jackson?" she asked, her voice carrying through the air and surrounding him.

He flipped off the faucet and downed the water in one

movement. Then he set the glass in the sink and turned. "I was thirsty," he said before he could stop himself.

Isabel had changed into a white polo shirt with the logo for Humanitarian Hearts stitched across the right breast pocket. It was tucked into her jeans, and her hair was pulled up into a loose ponytail.

She looked just the same and yet more beautiful than he remembered. Maybe he'd forgotten how beautiful she actually was in order to protect himself. Convincing himself that she wasn't as perfect as she had seemed was the only way he'd managed to put her behind him these past eight years.

She passed by him in the kitchen and grabbed her purse, shoving her phone into it. "Well, this kitchen is always open to you," she said as she slung her purse onto her shoulder. "Mom always said that." Her eyes glistened with tears, and Jackson saw her throat tense as she swallowed.

Mrs. Andrews passed away when they were twelve, and despite what Mr. Andrews thought of him, Mrs. Andrews had actually liked him. Hearing Isabel talk about her caused his chest to tighten with memories.

Isabel cleared her throat and pulled open the fridge to grab a can of sparkling water. That's when he realized that he was staring at her. He'd walked into her house uninvited, and Isabel's first reaction was to tell him this was a place he would always be welcome. Sure, Mrs. Andrews had told him their door was always open, but that didn't mean Isabel had to.

Isabel sighed and met his gaze like she knew what he'd

been thinking. And, honestly, he wouldn't put it past her. She always seemed to know. "We were friends once, right?" she asked.

Jackson swallowed as he nodded. "Right."

She shrugged and waved for him to follow her to the front door. "No reason why we can't remain friends. After all, I'm engaged, and I'm pretty sure you have someone in New York who is waiting for you to come back." She pulled the door open and stepped outside, only to stop as the sticky afternoon air surrounded them.

Startled, Jackson didn't have time to stop, and he ran straight into her. Worried he'd knock her over, he reached out and grabbed ahold of her arms. Warmth cascaded across his palms and up his arms as the familiarity of her skin against his own assaulted his senses.

She looked as startled as he felt as she raised her gaze up to meet his. It felt like an eternity passed between them as he held onto her. It was like his body had finally gotten her back and wasn't sure it wanted to let her go again.

His hesitation mixed with the depth in her gaze and froze Jackson in his spot.

"I need to grab something," she breathed.

That seemed to snap Jackson from his trance. He dropped his hands like the warmth of her skin had burned him and stepped out of the way.

He certainly wasn't acting like a guy who had moved on from his high school girlfriend. Not wanting her to get the wrong idea—or maybe the right one—Jackson shoved his hands through his hair and then into his front pockets, hoping to squelch his desire to touch her again.

She was engaged and very much off limits. He needed to remember that.

"Right, sorry," he said.

Isabel gave him a small smile as she maneuvered past him and headed back toward the kitchen. A few seconds later, she returned with her drink, which she waved in front of him.

He held the door open for her as she passed through. Once she was a safe distance away, he shut the door behind them, locked it with the spare, and then slipped the key back under the gnome.

"You remembered?" she asked.

Jackson straightened and turned, shooting her a sheepish look. "I took a guess that it was still there. Looks like some things never change." He held her gaze for a moment as the weight of his words settled around him. He cleared his throat and nodded toward his car. "Can I give you a ride?"

Isabel glanced at the black Lincoln and then squinted back at him. "Do you think it's safe?"

Not sure if she meant their relationship or his driving, Jackson shrugged. "It'll be fine. Besides, I want to say hi to Dean." To emphasize how fine he was about this, Jackson threw his keys up into the air as he made his way toward the driver's door.

He held his breath as he slipped into the seat and shoved

the key into the ignition. He wasn't sure if Isabel was going to follow, and relief flooded his body when he heard the passenger door open.

She shut the door and wrapped her hands around her purse. Her lips were pressed together as she stared at the dash. "Thanks," she said as Jackson started up the engine.

He threw the car into reverse and backed out of the driveway. "Of course. Besides, I'm pretty sure my mom would tan my hide if she found out I left you stranded."

Isabel's chuckle turned into a full-blown laugh, pure and uninhibited. It filled the air in the car, washing over Jackson like the waves of the ocean.

It sounded amazing—just like he remembered. This was the Isabel he knew. Not the fake one she'd been putting on for him earlier. This was perfection.

Isabel smiled. "Your mom. I've missed her."

Jackson rolled to a stop at a red light. "I'm surprised. Has Honey Grove gotten bigger since I left?" He peered down the familiar downtown streets.

Isabel shook her head. "No. I've just been...busy."

Jackson nodded. He didn't need her reminding him that she was getting married. That her new life was about to start while his was wavering over a chasm of uncertainty.

"Is he nice?" Before he could stop himself, the ridiculous question rattled off his tongue.

He saw Isabel glance over at him with her eyebrows furrowed. A sharp honk sounded from behind them, and Jackson glanced up to see the light had turned green.

"Who?" she asked.

"Your fiancé?"

She nodded—a bit too quickly—as she worried her hands. "Right. Bobby." She sighed. It wasn't the soft, in-love sound he'd expected. No, this was more reserved. "Yes. He's nice. Dad loves him."

Frustration coursed through Jackson at the mention of Mr. Andrews. He gripped the wheel as his knuckles turned white. Of course, he liked *Bobby*. Why wouldn't he?

Suddenly, all Jackson could think about was meeting the guy. Seeing what kind of person Mr. Andrews finally deemed worthy of his daughter's hand. "I'd like the meet him," Jackson said and then winced.

Why did his voice have to give him away like that?

The air fell silent. Confused, Jackson glanced over to find Isabel with her lips pinched together. She had a pained expression on her face like he'd struck a nerve.

"I'm sorry," he said, worried he'd crossed a line—he just wasn't sure what line that was.

Isabel shook her head. "No, it's fine. There's nothing to apologize for." She turned and gave him a forced smile. "I'd love for you to meet Bobby, he's just not here right now. He's out of town on business."

Jackson pulled to a stop outside of Humanitarian Hearts. It was sandwiched between an ice cream parlor and a bakery on Main street. Dean, Jackson's foster brother, had started it five years ago when he discovered that his birth mom had died from an overdose.

Dean was probably the most selfless person Jackson knew. It boggled his mind that Dean deemed him worthy of his friendship.

But what Isabel had just said was rattling around in Jackson's mind. "He's gone? Two weeks before the wedding?"

Isabel nodded as she pushed her door open. "Yeah, but it's fine. I have everything under control."

Was this what was bothering her so much? The fact that her wedding was days away and yet her fiancé was gone? "Isabel," Jackson said, reaching out and wrapping his hand around her forearm, halting her retreat.

She hesitated a moment and then turned to face him. She gave him a pleading smile. "I'm fine, Jackson, really. I've got everything handled. I'm pretty much just waiting for the big day myself."

Jackson furrowed his brows. He knew she was lying. The usual telltale signs were written all over her face. From the tremor in her bottom lip to the wrinkle that appeared between her brows.

She was very much not okay.

"Isabel—"

But before he could finish, she held up her hand. "Please, Jackson. Don't." She shot him a pleading look, and he couldn't help but pinch his lips closed.

He hated that she was hurting. After all these years, all he wanted to do was make her happy. To take away her pain. So instead of pushing the issue, he just nodded.

Isabel blew out her breath as she climbed out of the car. "I'll see you around?" she asked, dipping down to meet his gaze.

Jackson just nodded. He wasn't planning to stick around past Jonathan's wedding, but it didn't feel right to mention that right then. Instead, he waved as she slammed the door and hurried to the entrance of the building. He waited a few minutes before he climbed out of the car and headed in after her.

He wanted to give her space and time to get situated. When he got inside, he just wanted to find Dean and lose himself in talking with his best friend and foster brother.

'Cause right now, he needed to lose himself before he was consumed by the feelings he'd been convinced were dead all these years.

He'd gotten over Isabel once—he wasn't sure if he could do it again.

FOUR

ISABEL

ISABEL LET OUT her breath as she entered the kitchen of Humanitarian Hearts. She didn't like the way her heart was pounding or the way Jackson's face kept surfacing in her mind.

She needed to forget him.

He was the past, and Bobby was the future. Jackson had a life in New York, and she had a life here in Honey Grove. And a big part of that life was getting her dad out of the nursing home and back with her.

It was best for her to just forget everything he'd said. Everything that had happened between her and Jackson.

She'd forgotten about him once. She could do it again.

She hoped.

"You look the worse for wear," Nancy said as Isabel passed by. Nancy was cutting carrots into strips.

Isabel snorted as she patted Nancy on the back. Nancy

was twenty years her elder but was still one of her good friends. "Thanks. You always know how to make me feel better."

Nancy chuckled. "Anything for you, love."

Isabel made her way to the back to stick her purse in her locker and then grabbed a hairnet and apron. She made her way back to Nancy, tying the apron strings as she went. After washing her hands in the nearby sink, she grabbed a knife and started cutting.

"Geez, hon. What did those carrots ever do to you?" Nancy's voice cut through Isabel's concentration. Isabel glanced up to see Nancy nodding toward the cutting board. "Want to talk about it?"

Isabel dropped her gaze to the knife as embarrassment coursed through her.

Maybe it was the fact that she'd just spent longer with Jackson than she thought possible or the fact that her car was broken and her meager bank account probably didn't have enough money to fix it. Either way, her frustration had boiled over, and she was taking it out on the food.

She sheepishly set the knife down and took a deep breath. Then she turned and smiled at Nancy, who was studying her a bit too hard. Like she knew exactly what was going on in Isabel's mind.

And since Nancy was basically a mother figure to her, Isabel was pretty sure she could see right through her.

"Do you want to talk about it?" Nancy asked again as she returned to the carrots in front of her.

Yes, she did. But Isabel knew the minute she opened her lips her emotions would hit their boiling point, and she would lose what little control she had. And a commercial kitchen filled with about ten other people was the last place she wanted that to happen.

Thankfully, Dean walked in before Nancy could push her further. Relief flooded her chest as she smiled over at him...until Jackson walked in behind him. They were laughing and joking—like it hadn't been eight years since Jackson had been back.

A dull ache took up residence in her chest she remembered the three of them spending sticky summer nights together as teenagers. They would eat snow cones and camp out under the stars. It was amazing how real the past could feel. It took Isabel's breath away.

Dean and Jackson didn't stop as they made their way into Dean's office and shut the door. Isabel swallowed, hoping to push down her emotions. She blinked a few times as she glanced down to ready her knife over a carrot.

"Jackson is back?" Nancy asked just as Isabel pushed down.

Her words startled Isabel, and the knife slid to the side and right on top of her finger. Isabel watched as blood welled. It took a few seconds before the pain reached her receptors.

She yelped and grabbed her finger with her hand, applying pressure to the cut.

"Isabel, are you okay?" Nancy asked.

Tears stung Isabel's eyes as she rushed over to the sink. She flipped on the water and ran her hands under it. The water turned red as the blood was flushed down the drain.

"Are you okay?" Dean's voice asked.

Isabel jumped and turned to see that Dean and Jackson were behind her, staring into the sink. All she could do was nod as a tear rolled down her cheek. She wanted to say that it was from the cut, but with the way her heart was aching, it was from so much more.

"I cut myself," she said.

Dean stepped closer and nodded toward her hands. "Let me see."

Isabel winced but brought her hands up and slowly uncurled her fingers from the cut. Her hand pooled with blood, and from the look on Dean's face, it wasn't good.

"I think you should go see the doctor," he said as he reached over the sink and pulled some paper towels free. Isabel nodded as she wrapped the paper towels around her finger and squeezed. Then she glanced over at Jackson, whose brow was furrowed as he studied her.

She shot him a weak smile and then located Nancy, who was still standing by the counter cutting carrots. "Can you take me?" she called in Nancy's direction.

"I can take you," Jackson offered.

Isabel glanced over at him and then shook her head. "It's okay. I'm sure Nancy can take me."

"It's really no problem. I was just headed home anyway," Jackson said, stepping closer to her.

His close proximity sent Isabel's mind swirling. She swallowed, trying to ground herself. It was ridiculous how he could still make her body react. He was her past. She'd gotten over him.

She'd moved on.

"That would be great, actually. I really need Nancy here to finish up," Dean said, obviously not noticing Isabel's discomfort.

Great.

The air fell silent, and Isabel realized that everyone was staring at her. She glanced around at everyone and then sighed.

"Okay. Jackson can take me."

Dean patted her shoulder and then handed a slip for her to use when she got to the urgent care center since this was a work-related injury. She nodded and gingerly took it between her fingertips. Then she led Jackson to her locker, where he helped her slip out of her apron and hairnet and gather her stuff.

Nancy shot her an apologetic smile as Isabel followed Jackson back through the kitchen and into the early evening air. He remained quiet as he held open her door so she could slip into the seat. She fumbled with the seatbelt, and Jackson dipped into the car.

"Can I help?" he asked.

Isabel wanted the ground to open up and swallow her whole, but knowing that was impossible, she just nodded. Jackson took the seatbelt and leaned over her, brushing her skin with his own.

Her body flushed at his touch. Her stomach felt light from his mere presence. He was only millimeters from her right now. He smelled familiar. He felt familiar.

And she hated and longed for it at the same time.

Once the latch clicked and Jackson straightened, Isabel took in a deep breath and vowed never to be that close to him again.

That way lay heartbreak. Besides, she was engaged. She couldn't have feelings for her ex. She was just so discombobulated from everything that had happened. And she'd lost a lot of blood—she was just lightheaded from that.

Not Jackson.

He shut her door and jogged around the hood. He slipped into his seat and started the engine. It roared to life and he grabbed the back of her seat as he turned to look out the back.

Isabel's breath hitched in her throat.

Frustrated and angry at herself, she shifted so that her arm was resting on the door and her body was as far away from Jackson as the car allowed.

Once they were on the road heading toward the urgent care center, Isabel allowed her body to relax slightly. The tension she'd been feeling began to settle, and she could finally breath again.

"How are you feeling?" Jackson asked. She felt his gaze on her and turned to see him studying her.

Her cheeks felt like they were on fire. "My hand hurts,

but other than that, I'm okay." She winced as a sharp pain shot through her arm.

It was strange. The pain from her cut was dulled by her reaction to Jackson. But when she actually focused on her hand, she was reminded that she had a cut on her finger.

"I'm hurrying," Jackson said. From the corner of her eye, she saw Jackson focus back on the road.

"Thanks," she said. It came out soft and vulnerable— just like she felt.

Blast.

"Of course," he said glancing over at her once more.

She shifted in her seat. Why did things have to be so complicated? Why hadn't time allowed her to forget what it was like to be with Jackson. Why was it constantly reminding her of everything she'd missed the moment he left?

She'd been hurt, but she'd moved on. At least, that's what she thought.

"I'm here for you, you know that, right?" Jackson's tone was low, and his words held so much meaning that the lump she'd successfully wrestled down returned.

Why couldn't he be mean? It was harder to hate him or convince herself that she'd moved on when he was being so nice.

Jackson glanced over at her expectantly.

"I know," she said, her heart squeezing. Truth was, she knew he was there for her. That's who he was.

He nodded as he pulled into the urgent care parking lot and killed the engine. "Come on, let's get you stitched up."

Isabel moved to grab her door handle. As she shifted to climb out of the car, Jackson was already there, waiting for her. He rested his hand on her door and extended his free hand. She stared at it for moment before she forced herself to take it.

They were on a good path right now. There was no need to reject his help.

"Thanks," she mumbled as she slipped her hand into his. Warmth spread across her skin and ricocheted into her heart. Her pulse quickened and her body warmed from his touch.

It was such a familiar feeling—her hand in his. It was calming. It felt like home.

Shocked by her reaction, she dropped his hand as soon as she could and focused her attention on applying pressure to her cut.

They could be friends, but touching had to be off the table. Especially when her body couldn't seem to remember Bobby. She couldn't let the feeling of Jackson's skin against hers fill the broken cracks of her soul, right now.

Jackson was off limits.

"Come on," he said, motioning toward the care center's sliding doors.

Isabel pinched her lips together and nodded as she moved toward the entrance.

Once inside, Jackson found a chair in the waiting area, and Isabel headed to the front desk. After explaining what had happened and filling out some paperwork, she was told to sit and wait. She nodded and glanced behind her to find Jackson had settled in with a magazine propped up on his crossed leg.

He looked so relaxed and at ease. Not a jumble of nerves like she was.

It was idiotic for her to be reading into everything. He looked like he'd moved on and legitimately wanted to be friends. She was the one who was reacting to his every touch.

Feeling stupid, Isabel shushed her emotions and made her way over to the chair next to Jackson. Once she was settled, she called the Italian Shoppe to tell them she was probably not going to be coming in.

"Thanks, Pat," she said, after her manager told her to take it easy, and that he would see her the next time she was on the schedule. Losing a shift meant losing out on money and tips. And that meant it would take longer until Dad could come home.

The dream of taking care of her dad was slipping farther away from her.

And it was breaking her heart.

She slipped her phone into her purse and sighed. Jackson glanced over at her.

"Everything okay?"

Isabel chewed her lip as she nodded. "Yeah." And then

she winced. She didn't even believe her own lie. Did she honestly think that Jackson would?

"Really?"

She turned to see him studying her. His eyes were wide, and she could tell that he didn't believe a word she'd said. But revealing her pathetic excuse for a life to her ex was the last thing she wanted to do, so she forced a smile and nodded. "Of course, it is."

Jackson growled. "Isabel Andrews, I know you. I can tell when you are lying." He reached out like he was about to take her hand but stopped himself as his hand hovered over hers. It was amazing how something that had seemed simple years ago felt so strange now.

He cleared his throat as he brought his hand back to his lap and grabbed the magazine. "You don't have to lie to me. I can help."

Isabel's throat constricted as she blinked a few times. Sure, he'd help—until things got hard and he ran. Wasn't that what had happened? She'd done something and he was too afraid to face it. Or maybe the thought of living in a small town with his high school sweetheart wasn't ambitious enough for him.

None of those thoughts helped her feel any better. And she wasn't interested in baring her soul to someone who would be out of here in a few days.

"It's nothing I can't handle," she said, moving her hands to her lap. Her finger began to throb.

Thankfully, the nurse walked in and called her name.

She nodded and hurried to grab her purse and head back to the exam rooms.

An hour and three stitches later, she walked out with gauze wrapped around her finger and a prescription for some pain meds and antibiotics.

She half expected to see Jackson's chair empty, but her heart pounded when she saw that he was still there. He was reclined in his chair, with his head resting on the back and his legs sprawled out in front of him. His eyes were closed, and his arms folded across his chest.

He'd stayed.

Why?

Frustrated with the feelings that were surfacing, Isabel walked over to the pharmacy to fill her prescriptions. Once they were in hand, she made her way back over to Jackson. She couldn't just leave him there. Not when he'd waited.

So she walked over to him and nudged his foot.

"Hey," she said.

Jackson startled, his eyes opening and his hazy gaze falling on her. "Hey," he said, sitting up and pushing his hands through his hair. "Sorry, I think I fell asleep."

She nodded. It wasn't fair that he looked so good with his disheveled hair and five o'clock shadow. She was pretty sure stress had added twenty years to her reflection.

"You stayed," she said, her surprise sounding in her voice.

Jackson cleared his throat as he stood. "Of course, I did. How would you get home?" Then he sighed. "And who knows what my mom would do to me if I'd left." He glanced down at her hand. "Get everything fixed?"

Isabel nodded. "Three stitches, but everything is good."

Jackson shot her a smile. It was genuine and sweet. "I'm happy to hear that." Then he glanced toward the sliding doors. "Shall we?"

Isabel nodded. "Thanks."

They made their way toward the exit just as a familiar voice called out to them. Isabel stopped and winced when she realized it was Sondra Braxton.

Isabel glanced over at Jackson—he looked just as shocked as she felt. Before Isabel had time to blink, Sondra was wrapping both of them up into side hugs.

"What are you two doing here?" Sondra asked as she pulled back, keeping her hands firmly planted on their fore-arms. Like she was afraid that one of them would sprint away.

"Hey, Ma," Jackson said.

Sondra shot him a look and then glanced over at Isabel. "I haven't seen you in a while, sweetie. How's your dad?"

Isabel winced. That was the last thing she wanted to talk about. Especially with Jackson standing right next to them.

Hoping to move the conversation forward, Isabel just smiled. "He's great." Then she furrowed her brow. "What are you doing here?"

Mrs. Braxton looked as if she were going to ask more questions, but then she shifted gears and waved toward Mr. Braxton, who was walking out of the exam area and into the lobby. He was holding a piece of cotton to the inner crook of his arm.

"Just a blood draw," she said, waving Mr. Braxton over.

"Everything okay?" Jackson asked.

Mrs. Braxton shushed him and nodded. "He's as healthy as a horse." Then she zeroed in on the two of them once more. "What are you two doing here?"

Isabel's cheeks flushed with heat at Mrs. Braxton's implication. "I cut myself at Humanitarian Hearts, and Jackson—"

"I offered to take her here," Jackson finished.

Mrs. Braxton moved her gaze between the two of them. The height of her eyebrows told Isabel she was very intrigued.

"As friends," Jackson added.

Mrs. Braxton clicked her tongue as she held out her hand. Not sure what to do, Isabel reached out and took it. Mrs. Braxton squeezed her fingers. "You know what would be amazing?"

Isabel wasn't sure she was going to like where Mrs. Braxton was going. "What?"

"Ma," Jackson said, his voice low and full of warning.

Mrs. Braxton waved him away. "Come to dinner tomorrow. You can say hi to the whole family. Everyone's in town for Jonathan and Tiffany's wedding." She reached out and wrapped Isabel in a hug. "It'd be great to catch up."

"You don't have to," Jackson offered, stepping into Isabel's view.

Not sure what to do, Isabel winced. She'd always loved Mrs. Braxton, but spending the evening with the Braxton family really wasn't what she would classify as moving on from Jackson.

But the hopeful glint in Mrs. Braxton eyes confused her, so she said, "Maybe."

Mrs. Braxton must have taken that as a yes because she clapped her hands and declared that Jackson would text her the information—or "whatever you kids do these days"—and then she ushered Mr. Braxton through the doors.

When they disappeared into the parking lot, Isabel glanced back at Jackson. He looked like he'd just swallowed a whole lemon. When he met her gaze, he offered her an apologetic look.

"You don't have to..." he said as he shoved his hands into his front pockets and shrugged.

Isabel nodded. "I know."

Their conversation fell silent, and the weight of the day pushed down on Isabel. She glanced at Jackson. "Can you take me home?" she asked.

Jackson look relieved as he nodded. "Of course."

Isabel followed Jackson out to the parking lot. Her mind was reeling from everything that had happened. All the confusing emotions that were coursing through her veins were making it hard for her to resolve to forget Jackson.

Forgetting him seemed to be the last thing her heart or her mind wanted to do.

FIVE

JACKSON

JACKSON SIGHED as he watched Isabel disappear into her house. His chest squeezed as he pulled out of the driveway. The time they'd spent together had him all out of sorts. His heart disagreed with his mind, and he felt as if he were being pulled in two different directions.

And after his mom's invitation to Isabel, it was clear his trip home was not going to go as planned. He'd hoped to put his feelings for Isabel to rest. To see her happily engaged so that he could finally have some closure.

None of that was happening.

Jackson growled as he pulled to a stop at a red light. Why had he allowed himself to get involved? Why had he allowed Isabel to walk back into his life?

In New York He'd done so well at forgetting the one girl who had stolen his heart. Now it seemed he was a glutton for punishment.

She was engaged, and her father probably still hated him.

Yep, he was a smart one.

Gripping the steering wheel tighter, he pressed on the gas and flew through the green light. He needed to drive. He needed space.

Just as he got onto the highway that ran alongside the ocean, his phone rang.

It was a South Carolina area code, but he didn't recognize the number. Not sure who it was, he pressed talk and brought the phone to his cheek.

"Hello?"

"Is this Mr. Braxton?" a female voice asked.

"It is."

"This is Honey Grove Towing. We've got an estimate for the repairs. It seems like you need a new ignition, brakes, and tires. The cost is about a thousand dollars."

Jackson swallowed, thinking about Isabel. She seemed distressed when she had to call in sick to work, and from the look of her house, a grand was not something she had just sitting in the bank.

"I'll pay for it. Fix whatever you need to so that the car is safe."

The woman rattled off a few more instructions and said he could pick the car up tomorrow around noon.

Jackson thanked her and then hung up.

The silence was getting to him, so he reached over and flipped on the radio. Familiar cords and melodies filled the air, and Jackson found himself relaxing into his seat. He leaned back, resting his wrist on the steering wheel.

This was what he needed. The expansiveness of the road, not the stifled feeling of the past that smothered him when he was home. Here, he could be free. Here, he wasn't failing everyone he loved. Here, it didn't matter if Isabel's dad thought he wasn't good enough for his daughter.

Here, he was just himself.

Jackson drove for an hour before he got a text from Josh asking where he was. Realizing that he couldn't spend his entire time in Honey Grove on the road, he texted that he was on his way and dropped his phone in the passenger seat.

Thirty minutes later, he pulled into the driveway of his childhood home. It was dark out now, the stars above shining through the windshield.

The windows of his parents' two-story house were lit up, and every so often he saw the shadow of someone walking by a window.

Even though he tried to tell himself that being a lone wolf wasn't so bad, he missed his family when he was in New York. And if he were honest with himself, he was excited to reconnect with everyone.

Being the youngest Braxton boy did have its drawbacks, though. While Josh, Jonathan, and James shared a strong bond, they had always been too busy to bother with him.

Thank goodness for Jenna, but even then, she'd always had her own thing. Jackson always felt like he'd been the forgotten child.

Jackson pushed those thoughts from his mind as he pulled open the driver's door. Once his feet landed on the driveway, he made his way up the porch steps to the front door.

He turned the handle, and the door opened, revealing his family.

Some were gathered in the living room, and others could be heard from the kitchen.

"Jackson," Josh's familiar voice exclaimed. Before he knew what was going on, Josh's arms were around him and pulling him into a bear hug.

"Hey, Josh," Jackson said, thumping Josh's back.

Jonathan and James came into the room with their arms open. In a matter of seconds, Jackson was sandwiched between his three older brothers.

What had started out as a friendly hug quickly turned into a wrestling match. Determined to finally win, Jackson took on Josh and had him down on the ground in a head lock while Jonathan battled for dominance with James.

"Boys!" Sondra yelled.

Jackson laughed as he let go of Josh, and they all four flopped onto the carpet. Sondra came into view with a very displeased expression.

"If you're going to act like animals, go outside," she said, pointing her finger toward the window for emphasis.

Josh stood and reached down, offering his hand to Jackson. "Ah, Ma. It's all in good fun."

Jackson chuckled as Josh helped him up, and then he

made his way over to Sondra and wrapped her into a hug. A few seconds later, Josh, Jonathan, and James did the same, smashing their mom with a bear hug.

"You're squishing me!" she exclaimed through her laughter.

"Let your mom go," Tiffany said as she entered the room. Jonathan obeyed, and shortly after, so did the rest of the Braxton boys.

"Geez, Jonathan. She's got you whipped already," Josh said, moving his hand like he was cracking a whip.

"Excuse me?" Beth said as she entered the room. Her hand was on her swollen stomach. Josh and Beth eloped a few months ago and were already expecting a baby.

Jonathan was the only one who wanted a big to-do for his wedding. Which Jackson was thankful for. One trip down was all he could handle.

Jackson laughed, patting his brothers' shoulders. "Sorry guys, sounds like the only one here who's not whipped is me." Jackson plopped down on the couch and brought his feet up onto the coffee table.

"Excuse me?" Sondra asked, reaching over to swat at his feet.

Jackson's brothers let out a low laugh.

"You just wait," James said as Layla emerged from the kitchen with a cookie in hand. She made her way over to James, who'd sat on the recliner, and settled down on his lap. James's hand rested protectively on her stomach, and Jackson couldn't help but see how happy his brother was.

Whatever Layla was doing for James's PTSD, it was working. Jackson had never seen his brother so calm and at ease.

"Where've you been all day, little brother?" Josh asked as he plopped down next to Jackson.

Jackson glanced over as Isabel rushed into his mind. The thought of her alone in her empty house pulled at his emotions. He hated that she was by herself, and he wondered where her dad had gone and where her fiancé was. If it were him, he'd never leave her alone like that.

He'd done it once. He knew what it was like.

"Hello?" Josh asked, snapping his fingers in front of Jackson's face.

Jackson blinked a few times, forcing himself back to reality. "Sorry. I, um, was helping out a friend."

Sondra snorted. "By 'friend' he means Isabel Andrews."

Everyone let out an obnoxious "*Ooo.*"

Jackson hated how his skin heated. "It wasn't like that. She needed help, so I helped."

Dean had wandered into the room, and Jackson shot him a desperate look. "Right, Dean?"

Dean glanced around at them and then back to Jackson. "What are you guys talking about?"

"Jackson's reunion with Isabel," Tiffany offered as she settled down in front of Jonathan, draping her arm over his knee.

"His what?" Dean asked, looking completely confused.

"Jackson and Isabel?" Tiffany tried again.

It took a moment before Dean nodded. "Oh, that. Right. Yeah, he was making goo-goo eyes at her the whole time."

The room erupted in laughter, and Jackson shot Dean a menacing look. "What?" he shouted, probably a bit too loud. The entire room burst out laughing again.

Frustrated, Jackson stood. He was trying to forget Isabel, and having his entire family thinking there was something going on between the two of them wasn't helping.

"I invited her to dinner tomorrow," Sondra offered.

Everyone's eyes were on Jackson. Hoping to play it cool, he shrugged. "I doubt she'll come."

"She should," Tiffany piped up. "She'd been holed up in that house by herself for too long. And her fiancé? He's gone more than he's here."

Jackson glanced at Tiffany. Her statement left him with so many questions. And maybe a tiny bit of hope. Which was ridiculous—Isabel had moved on, and so had he.

"Where's her dad?" he asked, hoping he came across as nonchalant.

Sondra appeared in front of him. "She didn't tell you?"

Jackson furrowed his brow. "Tell me what?"

Sondra took a sip of tea from the mug she was holding. "He's in a home right now. He fell a few months ago and broke his hip. He has Alzheimer's, and Isabel's been trying to get him home, but she can't afford the modifications to the house that she needs for him to be able to get around. Let alone the nursing help she'd need when she's gone at work."

Jackson furrowed his brow as his mom's words sunk in.

"Apparently, she wants to stay here with her father, but the fiancé wants to move. Poor Isabel is stuck between the two of them," Sondra said, taking another sip.

Jackson stood there, trying to process what she'd said. Even though he had choice feelings about Mr. Andrews, he never wanted to see Isabel struggle. It killed him inside that she was hurting.

"Now she's left to plan her wedding alone," Layla added. Jackson could feel her stare on him.

He glanced over at Layla and nodded. "Okay." He wasn't sure what else he could say.

Isabel wasn't his anymore. She was marrying another guy. It wasn't his job to make her happy, even though helping her was all he could think about.

Jackson nodded to his family. "I'm exhausted."

Sondra studied him for a moment before she nodded. "The apartment above the garage is cleaned and ready. I figured you'd want some space, and Josh is no longer there." She turned and shot both Beth and Josh a look. They just shrugged.

"I got married, Ma. I live with my wife now."

Sondra threw up her hands as she passed by. "You both could live there, that's all I'm saying."

Josh muttered something, but Jackson and Sondra were already in the kitchen. Sondra just clicked her tongue and made her way over to a kitchen drawer. She rooted around until she pulled out a key.

"Come on, honey," she said, nodding toward the back door.

Jackson followed his mom. They crossed the driveway and made their way up the stairs to the apartment door. Sondra unlocked it, pushed the door open, and then waved Jackson inside.

She flipped on the kitchen light and turned to study him. After a moment, she reached out and pulled him into a hug. "I'm happy you're home," she said.

Jackson patted his mom's back and nodded. "Me too."

Sondra pulled back but kept her grip on his shoulders. "I know things went south with you and Isabel, but I really think she could use a friend right now. Promise me you'll reach out to her?"

Jackson stared at his mom's earnest eyes. He knew she meant well, but she didn't know what she was asking of him. Being around Isabel wasn't smart. Not if he wanted his pathetically glued-together heart to remain intact.

But he nodded. "Of course. I'll reach out to her tomorrow."

Sondra smiled and patted his shoulders. "You're such a sweetie." Then she sighed as she dropped her arms. "All right. I should go. Have a good night?"

Jackson nodded. "Will do."

Sondra gave him another smile and then made her way to the door and shut it behind her. Once she was gone, Jackson went to the kitchen sink and turned the water on.

He filled up a glass and downed it. Then he set the glass next to the sink.

He drew in his breath as he rested his hands on the countertop and tipped his head forward. His whole body was tense, and he needed to relax.

A commotion at the door drew his attention. Jenna was dragging a suitcase into the apartment. She glared at him as she slammed the door.

"Where have you been?" she demanded.

Jackson held up his hands. "What?"

Jenna growled as she blew her hair from her face. "We were going to do this together. You were supposed to help me with Mom." She staggered over to the couch and collapsed on it with a huff.

Jackson chuckled as he walked over to her. "Was it that bad?"

Jenna covered her face with her elbow and let out a groan. "She reminded me that my eggs aren't going to last forever," she murmured.

Jackson grimaced. That was not what he wanted to think about. His sister's eggs. "Bleh. Don't say that."

Jenna nodded as she slipped her arm down to rest next to her. "Right? *You* get how wrong that is. But apparently it's fine for Mom." She sighed as she stared off into the distance. "I mean, Beth and Layla are pregnant. Who knows how long it will be until Tiffany is having a baby? Do we all need to be pregnant at the same time?"

She groaned as she slumped further down in her seat.

Then she glared over at Jackson, who just sat there, not sure what to say. When she didn't let up, he shrugged. "What?"

"You're so lucky you're a boy."

Jackson dropped his jaw. "Um, then you missed our interaction in the living room. Mom basically told everyone that I'm still in love with Isabel."

Jenna studied him for a moment. "Are you?"

Jackson groaned as he stood and began to pace. "No," he said, but even he didn't think he sounded convincing.

"She's engaged, you know."

Jackson shot his sister a glare. "I know. And I don't care."

Jenna looked skeptical, but after a few seconds she sighed and rested her head on the back of the couch. "What are we going to do? How are we going to survive an entire weekend with them?" She waved her hand toward the house.

Jackson shoved his hands through his hair and sighed. "I don't know. Just grin and bear it, I guess."

Jenna looked over at him. "Promise not to leave me hanging again?"

Jackson chuckled as he made his way over and offered her his hand. "Promise."

Jenna laughed as he helped hoist her up.

"Come on, let's go to bed. We need to be fully rested if we are going to survive tomorrow."

Jenna nodded as she followed after him, dragging her suitcase. Realizing he had no clean clothes to change into,

Jackson course-corrected and made his way to the front door. "I'll see you tomorrow?"

Jenna furrowed her brow.

"I need to grab my luggage," Jackson said, waving toward his car.

Jenna nodded. "Right. Yeah, I'll see you in the morning."

After a quick wave, Jackson shut the door and headed down the stairs. Once he got to the driveway, he made his way over to his car. After pulling out his luggage, he slammed the trunk shut and sighed.

If what everyone was saying about Isabel was true, he knew what he had to do. Even though it would hurt, she needed him. And despite everything that had happened between them, Isabel was his friend.

Even if his heart still wanted something more.

SIX

ISABEL

THE NEXT MORNING came too quickly. The sun beat into the room and onto Isabel as she lay in bed, trying to ignore its light. She squeezed her eyes shut as tightly as possible, hoping to make the sun disappear, but it was in vain.

Today was another day. It was happening whether she wanted it to or not.

Sighing, she flung off her blankets and stumbled into the bathroom. She turned on the shower, and the warm water hit her, waking her up. It felt amazing, and it was just what she needed to start the day.

After she was done, she wrapped a towel around her body and used another to pat her hair dry. Making her way back into her room, she stopped at her phone.

One missed call.

She swiped her phone on. Bobby had left a message.

She pressed play and began rummaging around in her drawer as Bobby's voice filled the air.

"Hey, babe. Machu Picchu is amazing. We got a lot of good pictures taken. I seriously can't believe you are missing this. I'll be out of cell range for the next few days but thought I would give you a call. I really can't believe you want to give this all up to stay in Honey Grove."

His voice grew garbled, and a few seconds later, the message ended.

Isabel sighed as she set her phone down on her dresser and moved to get dressed.

She loved Bobby—she did. He was perfect for her. Or, at least, when he was around. It seemed once Jackson left, no one in Honey Grove was interested in her.

Bobby had spun into Honey Grove in a tornado of smooth talk and adventure. For a moment, he'd helped her forget the stress that clouded her life. He made her feel...fun.

But just as chaotically as he'd entered, he left. He was never one for settling down, and perhaps for a while she'd allowed herself to believe that he might. But when he left messages like that, she knew he'd never want to stay.

And staying was all she could do.

Her dad was here and leaving wasn't an option. No matter how much Bobby wanted to take her away.

She called Bobby back and wasn't surprised when she got his voicemail. She updated him on the wedding plans—not like he ever really listened, but she felt like he should be privy to what was going on. Then she told him about her car and the fact that she'd been stranded. There wasn't anything he could do to help. It just felt good to vent to someone about it.

She told him she loved him and that she hoped he was safe, then she hung up and set her phone down on her dresser. She'd hoped she would feel better after leaving Bobby a message, but she didn't.

Groaning, she flung herself onto her bed and covered her face with her arm. She took a few deep breaths as the stress of the world seemed to crush her.

She wanted to please so many people, and yet, she was failing at all of it.

Tears clung to her lids as she dropped her arm and stared up at the ceiling. She swallowed, trying to push her emotions deep down into her chest. She could do this. She was strong.

That was what she needed to tell herself to keep from crumbling into a sobbing mess.

"Get up, Isabel," she said as she sat up and planted her feet on the ground.

She needed to meet with the caterer and cake decorator today.

Then she needed to head over to Humanitarian Hearts for work.

She had a life and crawling under her covers wasn't going to get anything done.

After dressing in a flowy floral shirt and dark jean shorts, she quickly dried her hair and threw on some makeup. Just so she looked human instead of the zombie she felt like.

After a quick glance in the mirror to make sure she didn't look like a crazy person, she pulled open her bedroom door and padded into the kitchen.

She screamed.

"Jackson!" She gasped, clutching her hand to her chest.

For some reason, Jackson was sitting at her table, sipping on a coffee. He had the paper spread out in front of him and was reading it. He looked so...relaxed. So at ease.

Like he belonged there.

Blinking a few times to dispel that thought, she adjusted her clothes as she walked into the kitchen. Heat flushed her cheeks. What was wrong with her? Why did she have to scream like that?

Jackson glanced over at her and then pointed to the coffee next to his. "I brought you this," he said, dropping his gaze back to whatever article he was reading.

Not sure what to do, Isabel just stood there. Why was he here? "I'm going to have to move that key," she said, walking over to the table and grabbing the coffee.

Jackson leaned back and brought his intoxicating gaze up to meet hers. There was a hint of a smile on his lips as he ran his gaze over her. If her body wasn't already on fire from embarrassment, she was pretty sure she would have burst into flames from the way he was looking at her.

"Mom was right," he said as he pushed his hands

through his hair. He was wearing a dark t-shirt and jeans. And when he moved his arms, his muscles rippled.

Why the heck was she staring at him?

Hoping to focus her attention elsewhere, Isabel moved to sit down as far away from him as she could get. "About what?"

He shrugged and took a sip of his coffee. "She told me you're a mess." He nodded. "I have to agree."

"What? I'm not a mess." She fiddled with her coffee cup, turning it slowly on top of the table. Blast that Mrs. Braxton. She was so nosy, and yet, so right.

Jackson snorted. "Yeah. Sure."

Isabel was barely keeping her life together, and it angered her that Jackson would just come into her house and talk to her this way. Who was he to tell her this? He'd left. He didn't have a right to say anything to her anymore.

Feeling frustrated, she pushed away from the table and stood. Then she walked over to the cupboard and pulled out a granola bar. "Is this why you broke into my house? To scare the crap out of me and then insult my life?" She took a deep breath as she unwrapped the bar. "From what I can remember, you lost the right to talk about my life a long time ago."

Great. The tears she'd been keeping at bay were pushing through. She cleared her throat and distracted herself with throwing her wrapper away.

Jackson was quiet, and the silence that fell around them

thickened. Why had she said that? It was only going to prove that he was right—she *was* a mess.

"I'm here to help."

Jackson's voice had neared, and she turned to find him only a few feet away. At some point, he'd gotten up and followed her.

She met his gaze and could see the pain that lived there. Was he hurting too?

She shook her head slightly. She didn't want to dive into that right now. Or ever. Jackson Braxton left eight years ago, and she was engaged.

She took a deep breath. "Why are you here?"

The cocky, joking demeanor he'd been giving off earlier was gone, and he just looked...worried. He glanced around the kitchen and then back to her, pushing his hands through his hair. "Mom was worried about you. And so am I." He shoved both of his hands into the front pockets of his jeans. "Are you telling me you don't need my help?"

Isabel swallowed, her throat tingling from emotion. It touched her that he wanted to help. And she would be crazy to tell him no.

But she couldn't spend more time with him. She couldn't.

"I appreciate your concern for me. And your mom's. But I'm fine. I swear." She raised her hand like she was in court.

Jackson stepped back, running his gaze over her again.

Isabel's skin heated, but she forced a smile, hoping he'd believe her lie.

"Are you sure?"

Isabel nodded as she moved past him to grab her purse and shoes. After she shouldered her purse, she slipped on her sandals and shoved the rest of the granola bar into her mouth. "I promise," she said around the food.

Then she pulled open the front door and stepped out onto the stoop. She reached into her purse for her keys, but they weren't there. She let out a groan as she remembered her car was broken.

Jackson chuckled as he appeared next to her, holding her coffee in his hand. He glanced over with a wide smile.

"Are you really sure?" he asked as he pulled out his keys and rattled them in front of her.

His half-smile burned her up inside. She wished she could say it was from pure frustration with him, but she knew that was a lie. And despite the warning bells going off in her mind, all she could do was nod.

"Fine. But this is the last day you play chauffeur. I'm calling the mechanic and getting my car back."

Jackson held up his hands and nodded. "Okay. Don't think that I love playing chauffeur. I'm ready for you to get your wheels back, too."

Isabel glared at him and then shrugged. Whether or not he was playing with her, he was leaving at the end of the weekend. She just needed to hold out until then.

She hopped down the stairs and onto the walkway as she made her way over to his car. She glanced over at him a few times as he kept pace with her.

"Is Jonathan okay with you missing out on all the wedding stuff?"

Jackson unlocked the passenger door and pulled it open, holding it for her as she slid into the seat. After she was situated, he shut the door and jogged around the front of the car.

He climbed in and buckled up. "It's a perk of being part of a big family. Lots of helping hands. With Beth, Tiffany, and Layla, they've got more than enough people to help." He started the engine and pulled out of her driveway. "Plus, Mom wants me to make sure you're okay," he said softly as he cast a sideways glance her direction.

Isabel dropped her gaze to her hands. She wasn't sure how to feel about that. But she couldn't deny the warm feeling that spread through her chest. The fact that someone out there cared enough to make sure she was taken care of... well, that was something she was sorely missing in her life.

"Hey." Jackson's soft voice preceded the sudden appearance of his hand. It just sort of hovered above her knee. She could feel his hesitation. Like he'd suddenly realized that touching her wasn't something he was allowed to do.

At least, not like they'd done so many years ago.

Worried about what he was thinking, Isabel glanced over to see him staring at his hand. Then, as if something snapped him out of a trance, he cleared his throat and moved his hand back to the steering wheel. His knuckles turned white from the grip he had on the thing.

"Sorry," he mumbled.

Isabel shrugged as she wrapped her arms around her

chest and leaned in slightly. "It's okay. No big deal. We're friends, right?" She shrugged and shot him a smile, hoping that would negate the strange vibe that had suddenly taken over the car.

Jackson nodded as he pressed on the gas. "Right. Friends."

Ready to move this conversation forward, Isabel waved toward the sign that read *Real Sweet Treats*. "Right there," she said.

Jackson nodded and pulled into the spot that a black SUV had just pulled out of. The only real parking in downtown Honey Grove was street parking.

After Jackson turned off the engine, he pulled the keys from the ignition and shot her a smile. "Cake. I love cake."

Isabel couldn't help the genuine smile that teased her lips. The flirty tone he'd just used was painfully familiar. To this day, she could close her eyes and hear it.

And it was one that she missed when she closed her eyes at night.

Swallowing hard at the lump that had formed in her throat, she shook her head slightly as she chanted, *just a few more days*, in her mind.

A few more days. That was it.

Then Jackson would be gone.

Again.

SEVEN

THIS FELT WEIRD.

This felt really weird.

Standing in the cake shop, he watched Isabel approach the cashier to ask about her wedding cake. For two weeks from now.

Where she was going to marry another man.

Jackson stifled a groan as he pushed his hands through his hair and made his way over to the display cases that lined the far wall. All sorts of doughnuts and cookies were packed inside.

He dipped down as he pretended to study the treats. But inside, he was trying to stifle the rise of emotions that was clouding his better judgement.

Why had he listened to his mom? He'd literally broken into Isabel's house this morning. Why was he letting what his mom had said about Isabel affect him like he had? Isabel wasn't his to save anymore.

She was Bobby What's-his-name's problem. Not his.

And yet, here he was, allowing her back into his life. He swallowed hard and straightened. Man, he was a glutton for punishment.

"Isabella, my love," a low, robust voice bellowed from behind the counter.

Intrigued, Jackson turned to see a portly man decked out in chef whites, opening his arms and waving at Isabel to come closer.

"Pierre," Isabel said, leaning over the counter and patting his back.

But Pierre seemed interested in a bigger hug. He squeezed her to his chest, lifting her off her feet.

Once Isabel's feet were back on the ground, Pierre laughed, the sound bellowing through the store, as he clapped his hands together. "Very bad news," he said, staring down at Isabel.

Jackson peeked over to see Isabel's face drop.

"Unfortunately, my shipment of raspberries will not be available for me to properly process them." Pierre paused, letting his words linger in the air for a moment. Then he glanced down at Isabel. "I cannot just slap some jam on my cakes willy-nilly." He folded his hands and rested them on his stomach. "So we need to come up with a plan B."

Isabel just stood there with her lips parted. Jackson

could see that her skin had paled. He recognized the look she got when she was overwhelmed.

"So what're our options?" Jackson asked, stepping forward and wrapping one arm around Isabel's shoulders. Just as a show of support. From one friend to the other.

Pierre's gaze flicked over to Jackson. "Who are you?" he asked, shoving a pudgy finger in Jackson's direction.

"Jackson Braxton," Jackson said as he reached his hand over the counter.

Pierre studied it for a moment and then gripped it like it was a fish about to slip away. "Braxton..." He paused, and Jackson could see the thoughts forming in his mind. "Any relation to Jonathan?"

Ready to get his hand back and blood circulating through it again, Jackson wiggled his fingers from Pierre's grasp and nodded. "That's right. He's my brother."

Pierre narrowed his eyes. "And you are marrying Isabel?"

That seemed to snap Isabel from her stupor. She raised her hands, effectively breaking Jackson's contact as she stepped forward. "Oh no. I'm not marrying *him*." She waved her hands in Jackson's direction. "He's an old..."

Jackson's ears perked up to hear how exactly she was going to describe their relationship.

"He's an acquaintance. He's just giving me rides around town until my car is fixed." Isabel waved her hands as if she were trying to wipe Pierre's words away.

Pierre just narrowed his eyes as he flicked his gaze between them. "Acquaintance? What does that mean?"

Isabel pinched her lips together and turned to look at Jackson. Not sure what she wanted him to say, Jackson just shrugged. "We dated and then broke up a long time ago. That pretty much sums it up."

Isabel's jaw dropped as she stared at Jackson. Then she turned back to Pierre, her skin bright pink.

Jackson would be lying if he said he wasn't enjoying this. It was nice to air out their past. Plus, he was getting a twinge of satisfaction from saying exactly what Isabel didn't want him to.

"You are ex-lovers?" Pierre asked as he stared at Isabel.

"Lovers may be pushing it," she said as she stepped forward. "I dated Jackson, but I love Bobby. He and I are soul mates." Her smile turned soft as she stared at Pierre.

Jackson hated that her words felt like a dagger to his heart. Soul mates? Her and Bobby? If he remembered correctly—and he did—she'd used those exact words to describe *their* relationship on numerous occasions. Whoever this Bobby guy was, he didn't hold a candle to what Isabel and Jackson had once had.

"Well, I wouldn't say it like that," Jackson said, stepping forward and readying himself to spill the truth.

Suddenly, Isabel's hand was pressed into his stomach as she moved closer to him. Startled, he stared down at her. She met his gaze and there was this pleading look to them. Like she was begging him to stay silent.

"Please," she whispered. "I'll explain later."

Jackson studied her, not quite sure what this all meant. But there was a part of him that could never say no to her. He nodded and pinched his lips together.

"So, options?" Isabel asked, motioning toward the example cakes that lined the display cases.

Pierre looked suspicious, but then he nodded and extended his hand toward a small room off to the side of where they were standing. Isabel seemed to know where she was going, so Jackson followed after her.

Pierre sat down on a rickety chair and motioned to the seats across from him. Jackson stared at the small chairs and the even smaller area that they took up. Somehow, he and Isabel were supposed to sit that close to each other and not touch.

Which was laughable. There was no way they could both occupy that space.

But Isabel didn't look bothered as she sat on the chair closest to the wall, leaving the chair nearest Jackson open.

Realizing that there really was no way he was going to get out of this, Jackson sucked in his breath and sat. Pierre pulled out a binder and began flipping the pages.

Lemon custard. Chocolate ganache. Pierre listed the types of fillings he could put in the cake. Jackson blinked a few times as he got lost in Pierre's detailed descriptions of each picture.

Jackson wanted to care, he did, but no matter how much

he tried to force it...he couldn't. And he felt bad about that. Especially when Isabel nodded and leaned forward, oohing and aahing at everything.

If what Jackson suspected about Bobby was true, then Bobby had left all the planning for this wedding to Isabel. So, if Jackson was bored, it would probably hurt her feelings. Which he didn't want to do.

"Pick three, and I will bring you a taste test," Pierre boomed, smacking his hands down on the table.

Jackson jumped slightly as the noise startled him into alertness.

After Isabel rattled off three fillings, Pierre stood and left the room. After the kitchen door swung shut, Isabel whipped around and gave Jackson a sheepish smile.

"I'm sorry," she said, shifting in her seat.

Jackson tried to ignore how her leg brushed against his, or the fact that his arm was resting next to hers. Her skin was warm and soft against his own, sparking all sorts of memories.

"For what?" Jackson asked as he cleared his throat and shifted in his seat in an attempt to create some space between them.

If Isabel noticed, she didn't say anything. Instead, she fiddled with the strap of her purse. "For earlier. You know, out there." She waved toward the counter.

Jackson followed her gaze and then realized what she was talking about. Their strange interaction with Pierre.

Not wanting her to worry about that—and silently praying that Pierre would hurry up so they could get the heck out of there—Jackson just shrugged.

"No worries. I've already forgotten it." He cleared his throat and threaded his hands together for something to do other than obsess about Isabel's closeness.

Isabel shifted in her seat until she was staring at him. "It's just that Pierre is determined that his wedding cakes only go to people truly in love. He's weird and picky, but he makes amazing cakes." The soft smile that appeared on her lips caused Jackson's gaze to flick down to her perfect mouth.

Even now, he could remember what it felt like to get lost in her kiss.

Realizing that he was staring at her, he cleared his throat and forced his gaze upwards. A part of their earlier conversation floated back into his mind. The part about Isabel and Bobby being soul mates.

Call him crazy, but he wanted to know. Did she really feel that way?

"Are you?" slipped from his lips before he could stop it.

It must have startled Isabel because her jaw dropped slightly as her lips parted. Her eyes were wide as she met his gaze. "Am I what?"

Well, he'd come this far, he might as well finish. "Truly in love with Bobby?" He brought his hand up and began wiping non-existent crumbs from the tabletop.

He wasn't sure what he wanted her to say, but he was

pretty sure that whatever her answer was, he wasn't going to like it.

When Isabel didn't respond right away, Jackson peeked up at her. He could tell from the way her brows were furrowed and the way her lips were pinched that she was trying to decide what to say. Which seemed strange. Why was that a hard question?

Feeling awkward, sitting there in silence, Jackson leaned forward. "Isabel?" he asked.

That seemed to snap her from her trance. She blinked. "Of course," she said, the words spilling from her lips. She shook her head and nodded. "Of course, I do. I love Bobby." She stared at the table for a moment before she smiled over at him.

He didn't know much about women, especially when it came to Isabel. For him, she'd been a mystery even back when they were dating. But he could always tell when she was lying.

Before he could prod her for more information, Pierre returned with small slices of cake. In between the layers were the fillings that Isabel had requested.

Isabel seemed completely content to eat and make small chat with Pierre, occasionally meeting Jackson's gaze as he studied her.

Spending time with her had opened his eyes to so many things. One of them being that she was just as broken as he had been when he'd walked away from her eight years ago.

Maybe she hadn't told her dad to reject him when he

asked for her hand. Maybe that had just been her father interfering in her life. Jackson didn't know the truth about what had happened on Isabel's side of things. And maybe he wanted to change that.

"Which do you like?" Pierre's voice was directed toward Jackson, pulling him from his thoughts.

Jackson glanced at the large baker and then down to the pieces of cake in front of him. Not being a sweet treats guy, Jackson just shrugged and pointed to the first one.

"The ganache?" Pierre asked.

Jackson nodded.

"I like that one too. Let's switch to that," Isabel said.

Pierre nodded and filled out a form. After Isabel signed it, he ushered them from the room, telling them he had cakes calling his name.

As they stepped outside, all the questions that Jackson had still burned in his mind. Walking over to the passenger door, he pulled it open and waited for Isabel to climb in.

He shut her door and jogged to the driver's side, then he buckled his seatbelt and started the engine. He waited there with his hands on the steering wheel, trying to figure out just how to frame his questions.

He parted his lips and turned to see that Isabel was staring at her hands, tears brimming her lids. Maybe it wasn't the best time to assault her with questions about her fiancé, so Jackson cleared his throat and his mind. There would be a time and place, but this wasn't it.

Not when her quivering lip was causing his chest to squeeze.

"What's wrong?" he asked, aching to lean over and take her into his arms. But that would be completely inappropriate, he reminded himself, so he kept his hands gripped together in his lap.

Isabel shook her head as she wiped away the tears that were rolling down her cheeks. She glanced out the window for a moment before staring back down at her lap. "I'm so sorry. I'm a mess." She motioned toward her face.

Jackson leaned over, praying there was tissues in the glove compartment. Thankfully, there was a box. He pulled a few out and handed them to her.

She took them and dabbed her eyes and blew her nose. After she was done, she cleared her throat and then turned, giving him a forced smile. "Thanks," she said as she blew out her breath.

Not sure what to do, Jackson just nodded. "Yeah. Of course."

Isabel dabbed her eyes again and then rested her hands in her lap. "I'm sorry you had to see that."

Jackson shrugged. "I've seen you cry before."

Isabel studied him for a moment as if the same memories that were floating through his mind were floating through hers. "Yeah, I guess you have."

Trying to break up some of the tension, Jackson entwined his fingers and pushed them out like he was cracking his knuckles. "It's not something I can't handle."

Isabel dropped her jaw and swatted at his arm. "Hey, I wasn't that bad."

Jackson returned her shocked expression. "Not that bad? Remember Tickles?"

Isabel narrowed her eyes. "I knew you were going to bring that up. He was my turtle, and you took him for a swim in the lake. What was I supposed to do?"

"We found him."

Isabel laughed. It was light and genuine. And it felt amazing to hear. No memory could compare to that sound.

Not sure if he should be honest, Jackson decided to confess to her the truth about the story. "Or we found what I thought was Tickles."

Isabel whipped her gaze over to him. "What?" Then, as realization snuck in, she swatted him again. "You didn't! You swore it was Tickles."

Jackson laughed and moved to protect his arm from her attacks. "Hey, I was ten. What did I know about finding turtles?" Then he leaned in toward her. "He was your turtle. I figured you'd know if it was him."

Isabel's laugh subsided to a soft smile as she mulled over his words. Then she nodded. "Yeah, you're probably right. To tell you the truth, I didn't really know either. It was just sweet that you cared enough to lie." She peeked over at him through her long lashes.

Feelings burned inside Jackson's chest and stomach. Feelings that he'd told himself didn't exist anymore.

Which was another lie.

Right now, sitting next to Isabel, hearing her laugh, and feeling her gaze on him, he realized that he'd never really gotten over her.

Too bad she was already taken.

EIGHT

ISABEL

THE SILENCE in the car took on a more relaxed vibe. For the first time since she was reunited with Jackson, Isabel felt as if she could breathe. And if she were honest with herself, it was quite refreshing.

This was what she remembered. This peace she felt whenever she was around Jackson. It was like all of her troubles didn't matter anymore. All that mattered was Jackson and her.

She closed her eyes for a moment as she tried to focus her mind back to their earlier conversation about Bobby. Why had she hesitated? Why had her body picked that moment to have a major brain spasm?

She loved Bobby. She did.

But why didn't she remember that the moment Jackson asked her if she truly loved him?

Because...maybe it wasn't true.

Things with Jackson were becoming more relaxed. The strange tension that had existed between them since he'd come back into her life was dissipating—if only for a moment.

Even though they were fleeting, it was in those moments that she remembered why she had loved him.

He was easy to be around and laughing with him was as natural as breathing.

Isabel let a soft smile emerge as she crossed her arms over her chest and stared outside. The warmth of the sun shone down on her skin. She tapped her fingers on her arm in time with the ballad that was playing on the radio.

"Huh," Jackson said softly.

Isabel turned to see him staring out of the windshield. "What?" she asked, moving to follow his line of sight.

Coming up on the right-hand side of the car was Patsy's Parlor. They'd hung out at the ice cream joint basically every weekend night the summer before their senior year. It was quaint and sweet, with the best homemade ice cream ever.

"I wonder if my picture is still up on the wall," Jackson said as he flipped on his blinker and pulled into the parking lot. There weren't too many cars since it was still late morning.

The summer before Jackson left, he'd consumed a twenty-scoop ice cream concoction in fifteen minutes. Patsy was so excited that she'd started a board, boasting that whoever could finish in twenty minutes would get the ice cream for free and their picture on the wall.

Back then, no one had beaten Jackson's time.

Isabel shrugged. She hadn't really had time to breathe these past few years much less go out to get ice cream. "I'm not sure."

Jackson turned the engine off and pulled his keys from the ignition. He smiled at Isabel. "Let's go find out."

Isabel stared at him and then looked down at her watch. As much fun as it sounded to eat her weight in ice cream, she wasn't sure she had the time. Suddenly, Jackson's hand wrapped around her watch. "You have the time," he said, giving her an encouraging smile.

She raised her gaze up to meet his. It was soft, and his smile was so familiar that she felt her breath hitch in her throat.

It was a look she'd never been good at saying no to. So she found herself nodding. "Okay," she said as she grabbed hold of the door handle.

Jackson quickly fell into step with her as they started in the direction of the parlor. It felt so natural, walking side by side with him.

It was something they'd done so many times in the past, and it felt just like it had back then. Their arms brushed against each other, and warmth cascaded up Isabel's arm and across her body. She shivered, even though it was a balmy seventy degrees.

Isabel crossed one arm over her stomach, wrapping her

hand around her elbow. That would keep her from swinging her arms and risk touching Jackson again.

His touch confused her, and she needed all her wits about her if she was going to spend the afternoon with Jackson.

When they got to the front door, Jackson leaned forward to open the door at the same time she did. This time, her arm brushed his entire chest, and she felt him hover just behind her. Like he was moments from touching her.

Her heart raced as she pulled away. She cleared her throat and rubbed her arm. "Sorry," she muttered as she peeked up at him.

Jackson was staring at her as if he felt as confused as she did. He shook his head. "It's okay. I don't break."

Isabel glanced at his chest, her cheeks heating from the memory of his strong arms around her. Whenever he was close, she felt protected. Even now. They weren't together anymore, but he still made her feel safe.

"I know," she whispered.

Jackson hesitated for a moment before he pulled open the door and waved her inside. "After you," he said.

Grateful to put some space between them and get a handle on her emotions that ran away with her when she was with him, she nodded and stepped into the air-conditioned restaurant. A few customers dotted the counters that jutted out from the wall and left a section in the middle for the waiter to walk down.

Isabel rubbed her arms as goosebumps formed. It was

cool inside, and the thought of eating ice cream had her insides feeling frozen.

"Ah, it's still up," Jackson said as he walked past her and over to the bulletin board, studying the photos.

Intrigued with who else was in the Hall of Fame, Isabel walked up behind him. Jackson's picture looked aged, the colors fading under the fluorescent lights.

His smile was huge, just like she remembered. His hair was longer then, swooping to the side. Her fingers tingled as the memory of running her hands through it came back to her. He looked so...happy.

She missed that.

Back then, they didn't have worries. They could just love each other. Now, every relationship she tried to have was so clouded in expectations and worry. Worry that she would ruin things. Worry that she'll never make her dad happy. Worry that somehow Jackson leaving had been her fault. That he'd found out something about her. That she really was just unlovable, and that was why he'd left.

"Ready?" Jackson asked from behind her. A warm sensation spread across her back. Startled, she turned to see that Jackson had placed his hand there as if to draw her attention to him.

It had worked.

She pinched her lips together and nodded. "Yes," she said, ready to get away from the picture of Jackson and move on with her life.

Her past was just that—in the past. There was no need to drum up old feelings.

Jackson led her over to their old spot—a booth in the very back corner—and dropped down onto the old, cracking vinyl.

Isabel sat across from him and set her purse next to the wall. Eight years ago, she would have slid in next to him so she could share his body heat as she ate her ice cream. But now, that would be inappropriate and very strange.

Jackson opened the menu and began to study it.

Feeling like an idiot for obsessing over things that didn't matter, Isabel focused on the menu. She scanned the items a few times and then sighed as she closed the menu and propped it back behind the salt and pepper shakers.

She didn't need to look at the menu. She already knew what she was going to get. Mint chocolate chip ice cream, two scoops. Same as always.

Jackson seemed to have decided as well. He closed his menu and propped it behind hers. He drummed his fingers on the tabletop a few times, glancing around the room.

Thankfully, some peppy, blonde teenager approached. She snapped her gum a few times as she wrote their order down on her little notebook, her ponytail bouncing as she nodded.

She thanked them, told them it would be a few minutes, and headed back to the kitchen.

As their waitress left, Isabel glanced around. It felt so familiar to be in here that it was making her heart ache. She hadn't realized until now, but the last time she was here was the week before Jackson had disappeared.

The week before he broke her heart.

"What are you thinking about?" Jackson asked, drawing her attention over to him.

Not wanting to dig up the past, Isabel shrugged. "Just how this place hasn't changed."

Jackson glanced around too. "Yeah. It's strange. You can be gone for so long, and yet, when you come back it's like nothing's changed. Like Honey Grove is stuck in time." He pinched his lips together as if he suddenly realized how that sounded.

It didn't sound good. "Honey Grove changes. Maybe not as fast as New York does, but we change. We're not some Podunk town in the middle of nowhere." Isabel hated the bite to her tone but couldn't help it. This was the exact reason she hadn't wanted Jackson to see her life. She knew he would think less of her.

"Isabel," Jackson said, his tone taking a serious note.

Feeling frustrated, Isabel kept her gaze focused on the table. She recognized that tone. It was the one Jackson used when she overreacted. Even though she knew he was probably right, she wasn't ready for him to tell her that.

A few seconds passed before Isabel raised her gaze to meet his. His lips were tipped up into a soft smile, and his eyebrows were raised.

She studied him for a moment and then sighed, feeling her frustration melt away. "What?" she asked.

Jackson chuckled as he folded his arms. "I wasn't saying that like it's a bad thing. If anything, it's been a breath of fresh air to come home. Like, no matter what, I can depend on Honey Grove." His voice deepened, and Isabel couldn't help the rush of emotions that flooded her. "I like it," he said as he focused his gaze on her.

Not sure what to say, Isabel held his gaze for a moment before sighing as she focused back on the inside of the parlor. Maybe he was right. She didn't like change, so living in a town that was slow to change was comforting.

If only she could slow time with her dad, then maybe she could take a moment to be happy. "Sorry," she said as she peeked over at him.

Jackson furrowed his brow. "For what?"

"For assuming you were judging me," she admitted, the words tumbling from her lips.

"What? Why would I judge you?"

Isabel pinched her lips together as she took in a deep breath. Part of her wanted to keep her feelings hidden, but the other part wanted to tell Jackson everything. After all, that's what she used to do—confide in Jackson.

A shred of confidence seemed to be all she needed. Instead of pulling back inside of herself, she allowed her thoughts to flow, no matter the consequence.

"I don't know, Jackson. You left and now you live this glamorous life in New York. And me? I'm here, still doing everything I did when you left. I was...embarrassed." The last word escaped as a whisper. She hadn't been sure if she should say it, but now that it was out in the open, she couldn't take it back. And that terrified her.

When Jackson didn't respond, Isabel glanced up. There weren't many of his expressions that she couldn't read, but this was one of them. He stared at her for a moment before he leaned in closer.

"Why would you think I'd judge you?"

Isabel's eyebrows went up as she considered his question a second time. "Seriously, Jackson? Honey Grove was never good enough for you. You wanted this fancy, glamorous life. But that wasn't what I wanted or who I could ever be."

Jackson leaned back against the booth and folded his arms across his chest. Before he responded, the waitress returned with their order, setting the bowls in front of them and handing them some spoons. They both thanked her, and she smiled as she walked away.

Isabel was grateful for the distraction eating gave her. She didn't have to talk when ice cream filled her mouth.

A few minutes later, though, Jackson picked right back up where they'd left off.

"I didn't leave because you wouldn't fit into my 'glamorous' life," Jackson said as he stared at his ice cream. His nose wrinkled slightly when he said *glamorous*.

Isabel hesitated mid bite. She wanted to believe him, but she was having a hard time accepting it. "Really?" she asked.

Jackson pushed his spoon around his bowl. "Of course. I knew whatever life I created, you'd fit right in." He brought his full spoon up and slipped it into his mouth.

Isabel stared at him. Did he really think that? If that was the truth, why did he leave? She parted her lips to ask, but before she could utter the words, her phone rang.

She glanced down to see that it was the nursing home calling. Worry flooded her body as she lifted her phone and glanced up at Jackson. "I should take this," she said as she began to scoot from the booth.

Jackson raised his eyebrows but nodded. "Everything okay?"

"It's my dad."

A forlorn look passed over Jackson's face as he settled back. "Of course. Go ahead."

Not having time to waste trying to decipher Jackson's reaction, Isabel moved to the far wall and pressed the talk button. "Hello?"

"Miss Andrews?"

"Yes."

"This is Nurse Dorthy. I'm here with your dad. He's a little confused today, and I think hearing your voice would help. Do you mind talking to him?"

Isabel cleared her throat and nodded. "Yes, of course. Put him on."

"Wonderful. Hang on just one minute while I tell him who's on the phone."

Isabel waited, chewing her thumbnail. Worry rushed over her body as she waited to hear the familiar, tired voice of her father.

He was upset, rambling about wanting to be home to

pick her up from school. Isabel had to remind him that she was no longer in school. Her dad was still confused, but she seemed to be able to calm him down.

After a quick update from Dorthy, Isabel told her she would call again soon and hung up.

Holding the phone with both hands, Isabel took some deep breaths. It was never easy, talking to her dad on the phone like that. It only reminded her how fast things were changing and how desperate she was to get him home. If she waited too long, he was going to slip away before she could pull him back.

Tears stung her lids as she blinked a few times, trying to calm herself down. She didn't want to be a jumble of nerves when she got back to the table. It took a few more deep breaths for her emotions to settle.

Feeling better, she forced a smile and made her way back to the booth.

Jackson was almost finished with his ice cream and glanced up as she slipped back into her seat. She could feel his stare on her as she pushed her ice cream around with her spoon, not sure if she wanted to talk about what had happened.

"Everything okay?" Jackson asked.

Isabel nodded. "Yeah. Dad was just confused. I had to help calm him down."

When Jackson didn't respond right away, she glanced up. He was watching her again with a confused expression.

She sighed, not wanting to really delve into the details of the situation.

She set her spoon down and grabbed a few napkins to wipe her fingers. After she was clean, she reached into her purse and grabbed a ten-dollar bill. She moved to set it on the table, but Jackson extended his hand, stopping her.

"Hey," she said, startled.

"I'll get it," he said, waving toward her purse as if he wanted her to put it away.

"It's okay. I can pay for myself."

Jackson shook his head. "No. It's my treat." His expression hardened as he stared her down.

Realizing that she wasn't going to win this battle, Isabel just nodded. "Thanks," she said.

Jackson paid and they both stood and started making their way toward the door. Isabel wasn't sure what she was supposed to say or even what they were going to do from here, but she did know one thing—as fun as it was to talk with Jackson, that's all it was going to end up being.

Talk.

In the end, Jackson was going to leave, and she was going to be right back where she started. With a sick Dad and a deep desire to make him happy.

Jackson was nowhere in that equation. She needed to remember that.

NINE

ISABEL

THEY WALKED in silence back to Jackson's car. Isabel didn't wait for him to open her door, although she did hear his grunt of protest as she pulled on the handle.

"Isabel," he said, his hand holding onto the top of the door.

He held it tight as she tried to gain control of it. She could tell from the determined look on his face, he wasn't going to give up without a fight.

"We should get going. The caterer is waiting for me," Isabel said, hoping to deter whatever conversation he wanted to have.

Jackson didn't drop his gaze, nor did he flinch from her words. Instead, he stood there with his gaze trained on her face. She knew that expression. He was fighting the questions that she could see were burning in his mind.

She didn't want to hear what he was thinking. She just

wanted to move forward like nothing had changed. She was marrying Bobby in two weeks, and Jackson was leaving.

That was what he was doing at the end of the weekend —leaving again.

She couldn't disrupt her life and wait for him to decide to come back and stay with her. She had a plan that didn't include him, and she needed to cling to it with all the willpower she had left.

Jackson was a leaver—period.

Finally, he released her door and rounded the car to climb into the driver's seat. But, when Jackson didn't start driving, she turned her body toward him, giving him her full attention.

"What, Jackson?" she asked, annoyance causing heat to prick her skin.

Jackson stared at her a moment longer before he let out his breath like he was releasing something heavy from his shoulders. "Where's your dad?" he asked as he leaned forward and shifted the car into reverse.

Jackson's question shocked Isabel for a moment. That wasn't what she'd expected him to ask. Nothing about Bobby. Nothing about their failed relationship. Just a question about Dad.

And questions about Dad were things she could answer.

It was a strange sensation as her body let go of the tension she'd felt as she'd prepared to justify and defend her relationship with Bobby. Her muscles ached as she relaxed back into her seat and blew out her breath.

"He's in a home," she said softly. It hurt, saying those words. Especially since it was her job to take care of him.

When Jackson didn't say anything, she peeked over at him. He was studying the road with determined intensity. "What happened?" he asked. "He's too young to go into a retirement home."

Tears pricked Isabel's eyes as she nodded. That was the truth. Her dad was too young to have this happen, and most days she felt too young to be responsible for him. "He has Alzheimer's." The name of the disease that was slowly taking over her father felt like poison on her tongue.

Her heart was broken, and her soul ached for her father to return to her. But that wasn't going to happen. All she could do now was get her life together enough to get him home where she could spend the little time he had left with him.

"I'm so sorry, Izzie," Jackson said. His voice had deepened, and she could hear the intensity in his voice—he meant it.

Her heart swelled. She couldn't even get that kind of concern from her fiancé, and she'd wanted it. Bad. She needed someone to help her come to terms with what was happening, not try to force her to move on.

Bobby was a "move on, the outcome is already set" kind of guy. And he didn't realize what it was doing to her. She was breaking and didn't know how to put herself together again.

Jackson's hand appeared in her blurry vision. She

watched as he wrapped his fingers around her hand. His skin was warm and familiar and made her soul ache. Her body remembered what it was like to be held by Jackson and ached for that reassurance.

"Thanks," she whispered. Even though a part of her wanted to think that this might mean something more, she knew she couldn't look at it that way. Jackson was an old friend. He was showing his support like any friend would do.

They'd had a chance, and it hadn't worked out. There was no way anything could happen between them now. They were over.

Silence engulfed them as Jackson drove down the streets of Honey Grove. Even though Isabel felt hopeless, she was comforted by sitting next to Jackson as she stared out at the familiar town—the place she'd grown up. It held all of her memories.

And she couldn't imagine leaving. Not for trips to Paris or Machu Picchu. She loved it here. This was where she belonged. Honey Grove held her heart in its hands.

Jackson pulled into the parking lot of Holly's Catering and let go of her hand to turn off the ignition. Isabel tried not to complain when the cool air hit her skin.

She missed being close to Jackson. She missed their talks and how at home she felt when she was around him. She missed...him.

And even though she tried to remind herself that he was

leaving, her body was screaming that he was here, now. That she should take advantage of the time they had.

She just didn't know how to do any of this. What was being friends with Jackson like? What did it mean? What was appropriate to ask?

Not sure what to say, she parted her lips and said the first thing that came to her mind. "You were always a great friend. Thanks."

Jackson's shoulders tightened as he gripped the steering wheel. His gaze was trained on the dash, and she could see his jaw muscles flinch as frustration emanated from him.

He was hurting, but she wasn't sure why.

"Jackson?" she asked, leaning forward.

That seemed to snap him out of his trance. His shoulders relaxed as he glanced over at her, shooting her a strained smile. "Yeah?"

She studied him, wondering what was bothering him. But then she decided to shrug it off. When she began to wonder, she made mistakes. And right now, she loved having Jackson here with her. She didn't want to do anything to jeopardize their new relationship...whatever it was.

So she just gave him a soft smile. "Just making sure you're okay."

Jackson pushed his hands through his hair and nodded. "Great." Then he motioned toward the front door of the building. "I'll wait here."

Isabel nodded as she reached out to grab the handle.

"Awesome. This will just take a minute. I apparently forgot a signature."

Jackson nodded. "Yeah, of course."

Isabel studied him for a moment but then shook her head slightly and stepped out of the car. It was probably her oversensitivity to Jackson that was causing her to misread him.

He was a successful businessman in New York. A place that had women aplenty. There was no way he was still pining after her. Or that he cared what was happening in her life. She was just his friend, and she knew Mrs. Braxton wasn't going to let her son not take care of a friend.

The gravel crunched under her feet as she walked across the parking lot and pulled open the door. Cool air surrounded her. It didn't take long for her to sign the paperwork, and she forced a smile as Holly asked how her dad was doing and how the wedding plans were coming.

Not wanting to get drawn into a long conversation, Isabel kept her answers short but polite.

A few minutes later, she walked out of the store. She half expected to see Jackson gone, but his car was still parked in front of the store. She could hear the hum of the engine as she approached.

Glancing over to the driver's side, she could see Jackson had his head tilted back and his eyes were closed. She studied him for a moment, staring at the hard line of his jaw. His five o'clock shadow. His cheekbones. Everything.

He was so familiar that it hurt.

Isabel felt like a fool. Only a fool would get involved with an ex.

She was engaged. She was moving on with her life, and she was pretty sure Jackson was doing the same.

They weren't anything anymore.

Even "friends" was pushing it.

And from the way her heart pounded when he was around, she knew she was headed down a path that would only lead to heartbreak.

Just like eight years ago.

She had to call this off before she fell down that rabbit hole again.

She rapped her knuckles against his window. Jackson startled awake and glanced over at her with his brows drawn together. He stared at her for a moment before he rolled down his window. "Do you need my help?" he asked.

She tried not to react to the way his voice had deepened from sleep. She used to love calling him in the middle of the night just to hear him talk to her. His voice was gravely and oh so sexy.

Just another reason why she needed to run away.

"I think I can take things from here. You've been so sweet driving me around, but I don't want to be a burden to you anymore. Besides, I'm sure your family is missing you." She forced the biggest, most relaxed smile she could manage.

Jackson stared at her. "Are you ditching me?"

Forcing herself to remain positive, she laughed and

shook her head. "Of course not. I just don't want to burden you. You've got a life, just like I have a boring, yet busy one."

Jackson reached over and turned off the car's engine. Before she knew what was happening, Jackson had stepped out of the car, slamming the door behind him.

He walked over to her, staring her down as he towered over her. "What are you doing?"

Not sure where to look, Isabel stared at his chest. He was so close that she could see how deep of breaths he was taking. She was sure that if she reached out her hand and rested it on his heart, it would be pounding as hard as hers.

"Jackson, I..." She raised her gaze up to meet his.

There was so much behind his eyes, so much pain and hurt, that it took her breath away.

She took a moment before continuing. "We aren't good for each other. We just hurt each other in the end." She took a step back, hoping that the distance between them would dull the ache inside of her. She wanted him to stay, and that scared her.

Not only because she was engaged to another man, but because she feared what he would do with her heart. He could break it again, and this time, she wasn't so sure she would heal. Not with how she was failing at everything else.

She glanced up at Jackson. His jaw was clenched, and his hand was pushed through his hair like he was trying to figure out what to say.

Not wanting to hurt him, she stepped forward. "It's what's best for us. I'll go and move on with my life, and so will you." She stepped forward with her hand raised. She waited for him to look up, but he never did. "This was good, seeing you again. I think old wounds that never properly healed were finally able to scab over."

And that was the truth. She'd lived her life in the memory of Jackson. Of what they had and what they could have been. But seeing him again made her feel there was a better possibility for her to move on. And she looked forward to that happening...someday.

"Isabel, I..." Jackson turned his gaze up to her and lingered at her face. His brows furrowed as his words trailed off.

Hoping he wouldn't see the desperation in her gaze, she tried to get him to believe that she was going to be okay. That he could let her go. That he could let the idea of *them* go.

"You'll be fine. I'll be fine." She smiled softly.

Jackson nodded as he blew out his breath. He shoved his hands into his front pockets and glanced around. "Can I at least take you to the mechanic? Your car is ready."

Isabel studied him. She wanted to say no. She wanted to turn and walk away while she still had the strength. But he looked so desperate, like if she rejected him, he would crumble.

So she nodded. "Sure. That would be sweet of you." Then as she walked past him, she held up her hand. "As long as I can pay you for the gas."

Before he could respond, she passed by him and opened

the passenger-side door, sliding into her seat. She sat there, staring out at the parking lot as Jackson followed suit.

Soon, they were on the road again, making their way to the auto body shop to pick up her car.

Isabel was trying to convince herself that it was okay she was never going to see Jackson again after he dropped her off. They were officially over, and she could finally move on with her life. But her heart still felt as if it were hemorrhaging in her chest.

No matter how much she wanted to convince herself that Jackson wasn't a part of her life anymore, she knew that was lie.

And always would be.

Jackson was her first love. And her heart wouldn't forget so easily.

TEN

JACKSON

JACKSON'S HANDS tightened on the wheel as he drove Isabel to the mechanic. Even though there was silence in the car, his mind was reeling with thoughts. Thoughts about Isabel. Thoughts about what she'd said. And they were muddled even more by his ridiculous emotions getting in the way of the rational part of his brain.

He knew Isabel wasn't his and would never be his again. He'd thought he'd come to peace with that and had even moved on.

But now he couldn't figure out what he was supposed to do. How he was supposed to act around her.

They had been such an important part of each other's lives and walking away from that hadn't solved anything. He was a fool to think that he could remain unscathed after seeing Isabel.

He'd allowed himself to feel things for her again. Things he should have left buried forever. And now his heart was hurting.

Throwing on his blinker, he took a left and pulled into the parking lot of the mechanic. He put the car into park and unbuckled his seatbelt.

"I've got this," Isabel said, holding out her hand as if to stop him from getting out.

He stared at her, trying to control his frustration. He didn't want this to be the end, but when she was determined to call things off, what could he do?

"Are you sure?" he asked. Was he crazy not to want this to end? He'd forgotten what it was like to spend time with her. But perhaps he was fighting their inevitable fate. Maybe he was destined to leave with his heart in pieces because they could never work.

She chewed her lip and nodded. "Yes. I don't want to impose on your family anymore." She slowly raised her gaze up to meet his. "You've done so much to help me. I couldn't ask you to do more."

Jackson nodded as he settled back into his seat. Thankfully, he'd already paid the mechanic. He knew she'd never let him cover the cost, so he figured taking care of it ahead of that conversation was best.

Besides, his mom would never let him live it down if he didn't help her. And with her dad being in a home, he doubted she had a ton of money just laying around.

At the thought of his mom, he remembered that Sondra had invited Isabel over. He leaned toward her. "Are you still coming to dinner tonight?" He braced himself for her answer.

She fell silent, and when he glanced over, he saw that she was studying her hands. "I don't know, Jackson. I don't think that's wise."

Why? Because of him? Because of their history? Or was it because she was engaged to some guy who was MIA? So many questions rolled around in his mind and lingered on the tip of his tongue.

He wanted to ask her what was going on. He wanted to confront her. After all, their relationship had been built on calling each other out on their crap. They never sugarcoated things. It was something he missed about Isabel.

She had been able to see through him and had always known how to push him to be better.

But the Isabel sitting in the seat next to him wasn't that Isabel anymore. Something had happened. She'd changed. He just wasn't sure why.

It was like she'd given up. Not just on them—he wouldn't blame her if she had—but on her own happiness. It was like she'd decided that living this life in Honey Grove was all she was good for. That she needed to take care of her father at the expense of her own happiness.

And that was driving him crazy. He wanted to hear her laugh. To see her genuine smile. Because when she smiled, she lit up the room. Angels sang when she smiled.

And Jackson couldn't help but want to fix all of her problems so he could see that smile again.

He clicked his tongue, knowing that his mom wasn't going to take too lightly the news that Isabel wasn't coming. "You might want to think that over. You know my mom— she'll be at your place with half the town if you don't come."

Isabel glanced over at him and sighed. "Yeah, you're right." She grabbed her purse as she pulled open the door. She stepped out of the car and then leaned back down to meet his gaze. "I'll think about it. Tell your mom I'm a maybe?"

He nodded, and before he could say anything, she shut the door and started making her way across the parking lot. He sat there, watching her pull open the door and enter.

Frustration coursed through his veins as he threw his car into drive and sped out of the lot.

So many feelings were crashing inside of him. Feelings he thought he'd gotten control of. But apparently, all it took was a day with Isabel for him to lose his ever-loving mind.

He needed the feel of the ocean across his skin and the salty breeze surrounding him to calm his nerves. To give himself the jolt he needed to snap out of the trance he was in.

It was definitely something he missed while living in New York.

The ocean was calming. It had a way of surrounding him and giving his soul peace. And if there was ever a time in his life when he needed that, it was today.

He followed the familiar streets back to his childhood home. He'd run up to the apartment, throw on his swim trunks and grab his board —if it was still in the garage—and head out to the water.

As soon as he pulled into his parents' driveway, he parked and got out, leaving the keys in the car. If he saw one of his brothers, he'd invite them out, but he wasn't going to go out of his way to do it. He didn't want to be slowed down.

He took the stairs on the side of the garage two at a time. He pulled the spare key from just above the door frame and shoved it into the lock. The cool air from the small apartment hit him as he stepped inside. The drapes were drawn in an effort to keep the rooms cooler.

He set the key down on the counter and made his way back to his room. After slipping on his trunks, he headed out into the kitchen and jumped at the sight of Dean sipping a glass of water and leaning against the counter. His free arm was crossed across his chest, and he was staring off into the distance.

"Hey, man," Jackson said as he walked over and grabbed a glass of water.

Dean blinked and straightened as he turned toward Jackson. "Hey," he said. He almost sounded like he'd been caught. But Jackson wasn't sure why—he was basically a member of the family.

"Going to the beach. Want to come?" Jackson asked after he downed the water.

Dean's gaze slipped past him as he hesitated for a moment, but then he shook his head. "Naw. I've got to head to Humanitarian Hearts. It's my night to dish up dinner." Dean turned, setting his empty glass down next to the sink, and shot Jackson a smile.

Jackson shrugged and pulled open the front door. "Suit yourself. I need some sun and some waves."

Dean nodded, and just as Jackson stepped out into the late afternoon air, Jenna appeared from the back room. She was wearing a t-shirt and had her hair pulled back in a ponytail. Jackson stared at the door as it shut behind him.

That was strange. Since when did Jenna and Dean hang out?

Shaking his head, he forced that question from his mind. He really didn't care what his baby sister was up to. All that he could think about was grabbing his board and heading to the water.

Thankfully, Sondra Braxton was a notorious pack rat, and he found his board tucked up in the rafters of the garage. He pulled it down and headed over to his car, only to find that it wasn't going to fit. Frustration built up inside of him as he set the board next to his dad's truck and jogged up the back stairs.

"Hello?" he called into the kitchen. Female voices could be heard in the living room.

Sondra appeared, and when her gaze landed on Jackson, her smile widened. "Hey, honey. How's your day going?"

Not wanting to be grilled by his mom—she had a way of pulling the information she wanted from any unwitting soul—he gave her a quick hug as he scanned the kitchen for the keys to the truck.

"Can I borrow Dad's truck for a bit? I want to head to the beach."

Sondra pulled back. Her brows furrowed as she stared up at him. "What's wrong?"

Jackson stilled his frustration as he smiled down at his mom. "Nothing. I just need to see the ocean. It's been too long."

Sondra stepped back and swept her gaze over him. "Nope," she said, waggling her finger in his direction. "I don't believe it. You take to the beach when you're upset." Then realization passed over her features. "Isabel."

Jackson's chest squeezed at the sound of her name. It was like torture and pure perfection at the same time.

"I'll get the keys," Sondra said with a knowing hint to her voice.

He nodded, thankful that he wasn't going to be grilled about the woman who'd managed to break his heart again. Sondra emerged from the living room with the truck keys in hand. She pressed them into his palm. She didn't let go right away, instead, she kept his hand encased in her own.

"I know it's hard now," she said, her voice low and meaningful, "but things have a way of working out. Trust me."

Jackson swallowed the lump that had risen in his throat.

He hated that his mom had so much faith in true love. She'd forced the four Braxton boys to watch every Hallmark movie that released at Christmas time. She'd even put them into etiquette and dance classes in order to help them "win the girl of their dreams."

Well it was all fake. Love was fake.

It didn't exist. At least not for him.

The one girl he loved was untouchable. Her dad hated him, and now she had *Bobby*—a guy that both Isabel and her father had deemed good enough to marry her.

But not Jackson.

He didn't matter. And up until now, he'd convinced himself that he didn't care. But that lie was getting harder and harder for him to maintain.

And maybe he didn't want to move on. Maybe Isabel was the girl he was supposed to end up with. Maybe the love between them was a *once in a lifetime* kind of love.

How was he supposed to move on from that?

Frustration brewed in his stomach as he leaned over, kissed his mom on the cheek, and headed out of the house. Sondra shouted something, but Jackson didn't stop to hear what it was.

Right now, the only thing that would calm his beating heart was the feel of water across his skin and the thrill of the waves under his feet.

And he wasn't going to stop until he got there.

Then, and only then, would he worry about where he

was going to go from here. How he was going to pick up the broken pieces of his heart and move forward.

If he was going to survive, he needed to let the idea of him and Isabel slip away.

Once and for all.

ELEVEN

ISABEL

"I'M SORRY, WHAT?" Isabel asked as she leaned closer to the young mechanic behind the counter who furrowed his brows as he stared at the computer screen.

"It says here that the bill has been paid." The poor kid looked worried as he glanced back at her. "So, it's been paid," he repeated.

"But how? By whom?" Isabel racked her brain, trying to figure out who would possibly front the bill for her. Or who even knew her car was in the shop.

"I'm not sure," the kid said, dragging out each word. "I can go ask."

Isabel waved away his offer. It was probably Bobby. The only other person who knew that her car was in the shop was Jackson. And he didn't have any reason to pay her bills.

"No, it's fine. I'm sure it was my fiancé." She drummed

her fingers against the counter. "Can I get my keys? I'm late for work."

A look of relief passed over the mechanic's face as he nodded and grabbed a key from the board behind him. "Here you go. If you could just sign here, you'll be finished."

Isabel nodded as she scribbled her signature next to the "x" and grabbed her keys. As she left, she shoved her hand into her purse in search of her phone.

She pulled it out and glanced down at it just in time to see it start to ring.

Bobby.

Relief flooded her chest as she swiped to accept the call and brought the phone up to her cheek. Finally, her life could go back to normal.

"Hey," she said.

"Isabel?"

She nodded as she made her way over to her car and shoved the key into the lock. "Yeah, it's me. It's so good to hear your voice."

"What? I can't hear you." Loud rumbling sounds were coming from his end of the call.

"It's so good to hear from you," Isabel shouted into the microphone.

"Still can't—" His voice cut off as the phone fell silent.

Isabel glanced down at the screen and saw that the call had been dropped. She sighed as frustration rose up inside of her.

Spending time with Jackson had made her realize just

how alone she was. Her life had become a rat race, and she was starting to feel that no matter what she did, nothing was going to get better.

Just as she slipped into the driver's seat, the phone rang again. Glancing down, she saw it was a number she didn't recognize.

She answered the call, hoping it was Bobby so they could finally have a conversation that lasted longer than a minute. "Hello?"

"Isabel?" Bobby's smooth, non-scratchy voice asked. "Sorry. I finally found a phone with some service."

She let out her breath as she shut the car door and settled into her seat. "Hey. It's so good to hear your voice."

"You too, babe."

Isabel tipped her head back as she allowed the sound of his voice to wash over her. This was what she needed. This would help her get over Jackson once and for all. "When are you coming home? I need you."

The line went silent and Isabel glanced down—they were still connected. "Bobby?" she asked as she brought the phone back up to her ear.

She heard him sucking air between his teeth. Heat pricked her neck as she realized what he was about to do. He was going to let her down. Again.

"Thing is, I just got this great job opportunity to broker some real estate deals in Australia."

Even though she tried to stop it, a groan escaped her lips. "Bobby, I need you here."

There was a pause, and Isabel could imagine the frustrated look on Bobby's face. It was the same look he got whenever he talked about leaving Honey Grove and she talked about staying. "Babe, this is a once in a lifetime opportunity. I can't stay cooped up in Honey Grove. You know this."

Tears stung her eyes as she stared out past the windshield to the world around her. She knew what he was saying was true. He'd always told her that he wanted to explore the world. He believed that they only had one life to live, so why not do it to the fullest?

She had just figured, at some point, that his desire to stay with her would override his desire to leave. "You're right. I know. When do you need to be there?"

More silence. "Next weekend."

Isabel's jaw physically dropped. "That's our wedding."

"I know, I know. But imagine it, babe. A wedding in Australia! I mean, it doesn't get more perfect that that."

Isabel shifted in her seat as all sorts of emotions rose up inside of her. Anger. Betrayal. Pure rage. Hadn't Bobby listened to anything she'd ever said? "My dad's not there," she whispered. Emotions clung to her throat, causing her to sound weak and out of control.

"I know..." His voice softened, and she braced herself for the *but*. "But we can't live our life for him. I mean, he's taken care of. Most of the time he doesn't even remember you. Maybe it's time you start living for yourself."

That was the last straw. Tears rolled down her cheeks as a sob escaped her lips. "No."

Bobby cleared his throat. "No?"

"No. I can't get married without my dad there. I don't want to travel the world. I like my life in Honey Grove. I want to stay here." She folded her arm across her chest, hoping to hold in the pain.

"Isabel, you told me—"

"Yeah, well, you told me a lot of things too. You know I can't just pick up and leave. I've been killing myself to put on this wedding, and you're just going to call it off like it's nothing?" She was ugly crying now.

And the strangest thing was it didn't have to do with Bobby wanting to leave. Truth was, he'd left a long time ago when he chose his career over her. She couldn't really fault him for it, though. She knew who he was when she met him.

And now she felt like a complete idiot for believing that his desire to stay home with her would somehow, magically, take over his desire to travel.

But he'd made it clear that wasn't going to happen. Ever.

"Listen, it's a lot to take in. Maybe we should just put a pin in it and discuss it another time." Bobby's voice had grown soft, like he'd suddenly realized how upset she was.

Isabel just chewed her lip as she forced her emotions to settle. Memories of Dad and how excited he'd been that she was marrying Bobby surfaced in her mind.

Remembering the reasons why she was doing all of this helped calm her ragged nerves.

Bobby was probably right. This wasn't the time to do something drastic. She needed a night to sleep on what he'd asked. Even though she was pretty sure she was going to feel the same in the morning, it was only fair to at least consider his request. She could do that.

"Okay," she said, her voice breathy from exhaustion.

"Okay," Bobby repeated. "I'll call you tomorrow?"

Isabel nodded. "Okay."

They both said goodbye, and Isabel hung up.

After throwing her phone onto the passenger seat, she gripped the steering wheel and tipped her head back, closing her eyes and taking a deep breath.

So many feelings were coursing through her, and she wasn't sure which one to hone in on. All of it was killing her inside. The strangest part about her conversation with Bobby was that these feelings weren't because she might lose Bobby. Her real fear was that her dad might not live long enough to see her get married.

It had been her dream for him to walk her down the aisle. He'd given her so much of his life that it felt wrong to not give him this one father-daughter tradition.

And there just might be a chance he could fly to Australia. It wasn't ideal, but Bobby did want to marry her, just not here in Honey Grove.

If she could give her dad the moment he'd dreamt of, she was going to do it. After all, when would this opportunity come around again?

It wasn't like Bobby wasn't thoughtful. He'd paid for her car repairs. She had to give him that.

After dabbing her cheeks, she started up her car and pulled out of the parking spot. Her mind was clearing as her resolution formed in her stomach.

She was going to find a way to make this work. If it meant hiring a nurse to fly with her dad to Australia, then maybe that was something she would have to do. Right now, it wasn't her own happiness she was thinking about. Her dad had little time left, and she was going to make sure that every moment counted.

Even if hiring a nurse would mean draining her savings and delaying his return home—fulfilling this dream mattered more.

Her mind was so clouded with thoughts that she didn't even realize she'd driven to Humanitarian Hearts until she pulled into the back parking lot and turned off the engine. Thankfully, Jackson's car was nowhere to be found. She was pretty sure she'd had enough encounters with him to last a lifetime.

Besides, she was a mess and Jackson would know that something was wrong with one look.

And she knew that as soon as she told him about her situation, Jackson was going to poke holes into her already crumbling plan.

She couldn't have that. Not when her life was slapped together with duct tape and spit.

After she slipped her keys into her purse and climbed

out of her car, she headed to the back door and pulled it open. The familiar sounds of dishes clanking together and laughter filled her ears.

Isabel smiled as she made her way to the lockers and put her purse away. After grabbing an apron and a hairnet, she walked over to the sink, washed her hands, and slipped on some gloves.

Right now, the monotony of working at Humanitarian Hearts was exactly what she needed. There was no Bobby. There was no Jackson. And there was no confusion about how she felt about either of them.

Nancy glanced up as Isabel walked past her. She was stirring the contents of a large pot on the stove. Her face was red from the steam that was rising up from inside.

"Hey, feeling better today?" she asked as she dabbed at the sweat on her forehead. She blew out her breath as she stared at Isabel.

Not sure if Nancy would see through her lie or not, Isabel just shrugged and forced a smile. "Feeling great."

Nancy let go of the ladle and made her way over to Isabel. She wrapped both arms around her and drew her in.

No longer able to keep her emotions at bay, Isabel felt hot tears sting her lids and then roll down her cheeks. This was what she needed. For so long, she'd felt alone. It was hard, trying to be the person keeping everything together. Especially when it felt like everything was falling apart.

Nancy's hug helped her realize that, perhaps, she wasn't as alone as she felt.

"Oh, honey," Nancy said as she pulled back, keeping a firm grip on Isabel's upper arms. "Something's happening to you." She squeezed Isabel's arm. "Come on. The soup's almost done. It's just simmering right now. Let's have a talk."

Not sure what to say, Isabel decided to just follow Nancy, who led her to a worn love seat in the break room. "Sit," Nancy commanded.

Isabel nodded and collapsed onto the couch. Nancy busied herself with an electric kettle. While the roaring noise of the water heating filled the air, Nancy opened two tea packets and set them in two mugs.

After the loud whistle sounded, Nancy poured the hot water and brought the tea over to Isabel.

"Thanks," Isabel said as she gingerly balanced one of the mugs on her knee. She studied the steam as it rose up from the liquid.

Nancy obviously wanted to talk about what was bothering Isabel, so she took a few deep breaths, hoping to steady her heart and her mind.

This would be good for her. Talking through her feelings with a friend was just what she needed. It had always helped her in the past. There was no reason it wouldn't work again.

Now, if she could only make her heart and mind listen to each other, she might be able to figure out what she was going to do. Her heart was telling her not to pick Bobby. With every beat it was telling her that Jackson was the one she loved—had always loved.

But her mind, a very loud and dominating part of her, told her Jackson Braxton wasn't a stick-around kind of guy. He would leave. Every time.

Her heart knew that Jackson Braxton had broken it once, but she was beginning to doubt that he'd do it again.

And it was that hope, that ridiculous, naive hope, that was causing the ulcer to form in her stomach.

"It's best to start from the beginning," Nancy said, tapping Isabel's knee as she blew on her tea.

Isabel nodded as she shifted on her seat. The beginning. She could do that.

TWELVE

JACKSON

JACKSON LAY ON THE BEACH, his muscles throbbing. He'd spent the last few hours swimming and riding the waves. The sun was drifting below the horizon, and he was enjoying the feeling of the sand under his body and the sound of the water crashing against the shore.

As hard as this vacation had been, he'd been right to take some time to visit the beach he grew up on. It was exactly how he remembered it. Pure perfection.

He closed his eyes and took in a deep breath. He'd managed to push Isabel from his mind as he forced his body to swim harder and faster. But now her face flitted back into his mind.

Her wide eyes and perfectly formed lips. Everything that made her beautiful. Everything that made her unique wiggled its way back into his heart, squeezing it like a vice.

He cursed under his breath and sat up, grabbing a

handful of sand and chucking it across the beach in frustration.

"Hey!" A woman said.

Embarrassed, Jackson glanced up to see Tori Hodges standing in front of him. They'd worked together at the Hog Pit during high school. She was sweet and flirtatious, but nothing ever happened between them because Jackson had only had eyes for Isabel.

Tori's eyes were wide, and her jaw dropped.

"Tori?" Jackson asked, squinting up at her, just to make sure.

"Jackson?" she asked, leaning down to study him. "What are you doing here?"

Jackson brushed his hands off and stood. He walked toward her with his arms extended. "Jonathan's getting hitched," he said as he leaned down and they hugged. "And you know I'll take every chance I can to throw sand at you."

Tori giggled as she pulled back and shoved his shoulder. "Yeah, I should have known." Her lips were tipped up into a smile as she ran her gaze over him. "You're lucky. When Trudy got married, there was no way in hades she would have let me spend my time on the beach."

Jackson faked a wince as he held onto his shoulder. Then he laughed. "I think my sisters-in-law would protest if I tried to get involved. Besides, they don't have waves like these in New York."

Tori folded her arms as she rolled her eyes. "I heard something about that. You're a big executive or something?"

Jackson stepped back and ran his gaze over her. Her dark hair was pulled back into a ponytail, and her face was pink from exertion. She looked like she was out for a run on the beach with her tank top and yoga pants. He'd always thought she was cute, and he'd been right.

"What?" she asked as she playfully shoved his arm again.

Jackson ran his hands through his hair as uncertainty tugged at his mind. But he reminded himself of what Isabel had said. She was marrying Bobby, and that was that.

It was time he moved on. And with the way Tori was smiling at him, she seemed like the perfect distraction.

"Just wondering what you're doing tonight. I've got a family dinner that I do not want to go to alone." He shrugged. "Wanna come with me?"

Tori's eyes widened as she scoffed and then glanced around. "You want me to come with you? To a Braxton dinner?"

Jackson furrowed his brows. "What's wrong with that?" The way she said it made it sound nefarious.

Tori studied him for a moment and then nodded, her expression softening. "Nothing. Never mind. I'd love to go."

"Really?" Relief flooded his mind. He wasn't sure he could handle a night being stuck between his mom and Isabel—if Isabel even showed up. Tori was fun, and that was what he needed right then. Fun.

Tori nodded. "Yeah, of course. It'll be fun to see your family again."

Jackson grinned. "You remember the address? Feel free to come around six."

Tori smiled. "Sounds like a date."

Jackson studied her for a moment and then nodded. "Yeah. It does."

Tori gave him one last soft smile and took off down the beach. Jackson watched her disappear, his mind swarming with thoughts.

This was good. He was moving on from Isabel, and Tori seemed like the perfect candidate. Plus, there was no way he would have survived dinner on his own. Not when his mom seemed hell-bent on setting him up with the one girl that didn't want him.

So why did he feel so guilty? Why did he feel as if he were cheating on Isabel? They weren't together. She was engaged. That had become a chant he'd repeated to himself every moment he was with her, because it was getting easier and easier to forget.

All he needed to do was survive the night, survive his brother's wedding, and before he knew it, he'd be on the plane back to New York. Back to his Isabel-free life.

Just as he liked it.

Glancing down at his watch, Jackson realized he had only an hour before dinner. He still needed to get home and showered. Grabbing his stuff, he jogged over to the truck and threw the board in the back. After the engine roared to life, he backed the truck out of the parking spot and took off down the road.

The house was alive with voices when he pulled open the back door and walked in. Beth and Tiffany were standing over pots at the stove. They were talking in low tones as each stirred some concoction.

When the door slammed behind him, they both turned to stare at him.

"Ladies," he said, nodding in their direction as he passed by.

He loved his brothers, and he was happy they'd found the girls that they wanted to spend the rest of their lives with, but he really wasn't in a mood to talk. Especially since all of them seemed so ridiculously happy.

And that was far from how he felt.

Tiffany said something as he walked past, but Jackson didn't catch it. He needed a hot shower before he'd feel up to being social. So he just dipped his head, dropped his dad's keys into the bowl on the counter, and then headed back outside.

The cooling evening air hit him, and he jogged across the lawn and over to the garage steps, taking them two at a time. He found the key, shoved it into the lock, and opened the door.

Twenty minutes later, he was showered and dressed and was staring at his reflection in the mirror.

He looked like he felt. Like a mess.

Isabel was coming. Tori was coming. And the last thing he wanted to do was to deal with whatever was going to happen downstairs. What had seemed like the perfect plan an hour ago suddenly seemed like a giant mistake.

Having either Tori or Isabel at dinner was bound to be awkward.

On top of that, he was going to have to smile and play nice with his disgustingly in-love brothers as they doted over their significant others.

At least he had Jenna. Maybe he should just call the whole night off and spend time with his little sister. She seemed to be the only one who knew what he was going through. How tough it was to deal with the expectation for love that Sondra put on them.

Jackson blew out his breath as he mussed his hair and closed his eyes. He needed to get a grip so that he could focus on the task at hand. Surviving dinner.

After slipping on his shoes and spritzing himself with cologne, he opened the door and made his way down the stairs and across the backyard. The rest of the family had made their way out to the back patio. The smell of hamburgers and hot dogs wafted from the grill.

James and Jonathan were standing near the food, each with a beer in their hand. Josh was throwing a football to Jordan. And the three new Braxton women were sitting in lawn chairs, chatting.

Not sure what to do, Jackson grabbed a beer and headed over to James and Jonathan.

"Grip it better, Jordan. You'll get a better spiral,"

Jonathan shouted as he held up his hand like he was gripping a football.

"Will you let me teach my son in peace?" Josh yelled back.

Jonathan shook his head as he turned and met Jackson's gaze. "Don't you look fancy," he said as he opened the grill, and steam and smoke billowed out.

Jackson stepped back and took a sip of his beer. "Some of us still care what we look like," Jackson said as he nodded toward Jonathan's stomach.

"Excuse me? What are you trying to say?" Jonathan asked. His voice was joking, but there was a serious glint in his eye.

"Don't you even think about it, you two," Sondra said as she walked by. She was carrying a huge bowl of potato salad. Jenna was following behind her and caught Jackson's eye.

Jenna widened her eyes as she nodded toward Sondra. Her typical "help me" move.

Jackson nodded and moved to take the bowl from Sondra. "Let me help you, Ma," he said as he pulled the salad away. Sondra started to protest, but Jackson shook his head. "You've been working all day. Sit down. Put your feet up," Jackson said as he nodded toward Tiffany, Beth, and Layla.

Sondra glanced at her daughters-in-law and then back to Jackson. She reached up and patted his cheek. "You were always my favorite," she said as she let out a big sigh and sat down on an empty lawn chair.

Thankfully, Layla swept her away in conversation, allowing Jackson to escape and set the bowl down on the food table.

"Thank you," Jenna said as she followed him. She reached into a bag of Doritos and grabbed a handful. "Without Dean here, I have no buffer."

Jackson glanced over at her. "You and Dean hanging out now?"

Jackson wasn't sure, but he swore he saw Jenna's cheeks flush. Which was weird. Dean was like a brother to them. It would be weird and gross for him and Jenna to have feelings for each other.

"Yeah, well, since my big brother who swore to protect me from Mom has been MIA, who else did I have to turn to?" Jenna slipped a chip into her mouth as she turned to stare at Jackson.

His thoughts immediately turned to Isabel and Tori and the mess he'd created for himself tonight. What the crap had he been thinking?

"What? What did you do?" Jenna asked, leaning in.

Jackson shook his head and turned to grab a handful of chips for himself. "Nothing. Why?"

Jenna leaned over the table to meet his gaze. "You have that look about you. The one you got when you dyed the dog blue." She narrowed her eyes. "Does it have to do with Isabel?"

Jackson could see Jenna's mind working, piecing together her version of the story. "Jackson!" she exclaimed.

Jackson glared at her. "Will you stop it? It's not what you think."

"Oh really? How is it not?" Jenna lowered her voice. "Isabel is engaged. What are you thinking?"

Jackson stared at Jenna, trying to process what she'd just said. "Wait, what?"

Jenna nodded at him. "You and Isabel..." She raised her eyebrows. "You know."

Realization hit Jackson like a ton of bricks. "What? No. I'm not that kind of guy." He cleared his throat as he tried to redeem himself in his sister's eyes. "I don't steal other guys' fiancées."

Jenna raised her eyebrows as she ate another chip. Jackson held her gaze, hoping she'd realize he was being serious. Finally, she sighed. "Good. 'Cause I was going to have to hurt you." Then she fell silent. "Or tell Mom. That could be fun."

Jackson hushed her as he turned to check that Sondra was still engrossed in a conversation with Layla. It was kind of nice, having more Braxton family members. It meant more people to distract Mom.

"So, if you didn't do anything with Isabel, why do you look so guilty?" Jenna asked as she dug her hand into the chip bag again.

Jackson sighed. "Mom invited Isabel to dinner."

Jenna nodded. "Yeah, Mom told me. She also told me to get you two alone as much as possible. Apparently, Isabel's fiancé is a piece of work. Something about wanting to leave her dad in a nursing home and whisk her away to all these exotic places."

"She would hate that," Jackson said before he could stop himself.

Jenna didn't respond, and Jackson feared what she was thinking as he studied the cupcakes in front of him. Why couldn't he just keep his mouth shut? He was going to get himself in more trouble than he wanted to deal with right now.

"I invited Tori to dinner," he said, hoping to distract Jenna.

She coughed, like she'd inhaled some chip dust. "You did *what*? Tori Hodges? Why?"

Jackson shrugged. "No reason really. I ran into her at the beach, so I invited her." Jackson downed the rest of his beer. If only he felt as confident as he sounded.

He didn't really want anything to do with Tori romantically. It was easy to think that all he needed to do to move on from the one girl loved with was to find another, but that wasn't true.

And he really didn't like the fact that he'd turned into "that guy." He didn't like the out of control feeling that was coursing through his body.

Jenna sighed as her hand landed on his shoulder. "It'll be okay," she said softly.

Jackson glanced over at his little sister, grateful that she was here to help him get through this. What did he know? Maybe when he was home in New York, he would look back on this weekend fondly. He would tell himself that going back to Honey Grove was a smart decision.

But right then, he was regretting every decision he'd made. They all seemed wrong. Both the ones that brought him closer to Isabel and the ones that pushed her away. Each brought him pain, because in the end he was never going to win Isabel back.

THIRTEEN

ISABEL

ISABEL SAT IN HER CAR, staring at the dashboard. Nancy's words were flowing through her mind as she studied the numbers on the speedometer.

"I think you know what you need to do. Being with Bobby isn't bringing you happiness. Maybe it's time you call things off for a while. I know your dad. He wouldn't want you to be unhappy."

Isabel blinked a few times as tears threatened to spill. Nancy had nailed it on the head. Isabel was so unhappy. She was constantly walking around with a pit in her stomach. The feeling of dread that she was making the wrong decision.

Why couldn't she just figure her life out? Why couldn't things be easy?

She groaned as she gripped the steering wheel and tipped her head back, resting it against her seat.

"Because I'm an idiot," she whispered. Why had she ever thought that marrying Bobby was the solution to her problems?

Sure, running away to an exotic place sounded like a dream come true, but when she woke up, she was still going to have to deal with her life.

Dad was still sick, and she was still too poor to get him home. No expensive getaway was going to change that.

After a few hard swallows to get her emotions under control, Isabel slipped the keys into the ignition and started up the engine. She pulled out of the parking lot of Humanitarian Hearts and onto the main road. Just as she stopped at a red light, her phone chimed.

Glancing down, she read a text from Mrs. Braxton.

Mrs. Braxton: Just making sure you're still coming for dinner!☺

Isabel studied the text, her heart quickening at the thought of seeing Jackson again. But she shook her head as she responded. They were over. No need to keep breaking open that wound.

Isabel: I'm so sorry, I won't be able to make it. I'm not feeling well.

She hit send and then glanced up to see the light had changed to green. She pressed her foot on the gas and made her way through the streets toward her house. Just before she pulled into the driveway, her phone chimed again.

Mrs. Braxton: Oh no! I'm so sorry, sweetheart. I'll send Jackson over with some food.

Isabel's stomach leapt into her throat. That was the last thing she wanted. In fact, the idea of sitting in her quiet house alone with Jackson sounded worse than a loud and crowded Braxton party. Maybe she should just show up for a few minutes and leave. It would appease Mrs. Braxton and allow Isabel to move on with her life.

Isabel: No, that's okay. I'm actually thinking I might just need some food. I'll be there in twenty.

Isabel grabbed her purse and opened her door as she made her way up her walkway. Her phone chimed just as she'd unlocked her door and stepped inside.

Mrs. Braxton: Oh, lovely. We'll see you when you get here. There's plenty of food.

Isabel responded with a thumbs up and then dropped her purse and keys onto the counter as she let out a breath. Right now, she needed a hot shower and a change of clothes. Anything to make her feel more awake and more human.

Fifteen minutes later, Isabel was standing in front of her closet with a towel wrapped around her body. She was staring at her clothes, trying to decide on something to wear.

Reaching out, she grabbed a light floral dress and held it up to her body. As she stared at her reflection, she tried to imagine what Jackson would think...and then pushed that thought from her mind.

What was wrong with her?

Sighing, she tucked the dress back into the closet and then grabbed a pair of cut-off jeans and a white tank. Something that wouldn't make it look like she was trying too hard.

She pulled a brush through her hair and put on some mascara and lip gloss. Then she slipped on her sandals, grabbed her purse and keys, and headed back outside.

The drive to the Braxtons' house seemed faster than she remembered. Maybe it was because she was dreading what she was going to do once she got there. The Braxtons were a great family, but the last time she'd been to their house was when she was in a relationship with one of them.

Now, it just felt like she was intruding on their family time.

After parking on the street, she turned off her car and got out. She slammed the door and took in a deep breath as she walked up the driveway and toward the back. As she rounded the house, she could hear laughter and smell the meat on the grill.

She gripped the strap of her purse. Everyone was milling around the backyard. Jonathan and James were huddled next to the grill. Beth and Layla were standing next to them. Sondra and Jimmy were sitting on some lawn chairs, laughing and talking to Josh and Beth.

Jenna was playing a board game with Jordan. And Jackson? Her gaze fell on him, and she couldn't help but stare.

Jackson was leaning next to a nearby tree. He had his arms folded across his body and he was staring off into the distance as if he were in a trance.

Not sure what to do, she forced a smile and walked over to where Sondra and Jimmy were sitting. Even though her whole body wanted her to walk over to Jackson—apparently, that's where she felt the safest—she decided that would be a stupid decision.

Announcing her presence to Mrs. Braxton felt like the right move. That way she'd be seen, and Sondra wouldn't feel the need to send any of her sons to stop by the house with food.

"Isabel!" Mrs. Braxton exclaimed as she stood and pulled Isabel into a hug. "I'm so glad you made it." Mrs. Braxton pulled back. "How are you feeling? Better?"

Isabel nodded. "Yes. Thanks. I'm just...tried." And that was the truth.

Mrs. Braxton nodded. "Of course. You poor thing. All alone in your house." She wrapped her arm around Isabel's shoulders and started moving her toward the food table. "Let's fill you up. Jackson?"

Isabel winced at the sound of his name. She should have known that within seconds of being here, Mrs. Braxton would push her and Jackson together.

Isabel snuck a look in Jackson's direction. He was staring at his mom and looked as uncomfortable as she felt. Not sure how to interpret that, Isabel figured it was best to just drop her gaze and focus on the grass.

"Come help get Isabel some food," Mrs. Braxton said, waving Jackson over.

Isabel hesitated, not sure if she wanted to peek to see what Jackson was going to do. Part of her wanted him to come over, the other part wanted him to stay exactly where he was. If he refused to come over, at least this whole weird experience would be over faster.

"Okay," Jackson said, his voice sounding closer now.

Isabel glanced up to see him standing a few feet away. His jaw muscles were clenched as he stared at his mom. If Mrs. Braxton noticed, she didn't say anything. She handed him a plate and waved toward the food. "Fill it up for her. James?"

James glanced in their direction.

"Get Isabel a hamburger."

James nodded and opened the grill. A few seconds later, he walked over with a steaming hot hamburger patty on his spatula. Jackson had readied a bun, and before Isabel knew what was happening, Jackson was filling her plate with food.

Isabel watched, not sure what to say or how to say it. Jackson put everything she loved and would have served herself onto the plate. Even after all of these years, he remembered what she liked.

When he was done, he straightened and glanced down at her. "I'll get you a soda. Why don't you find a seat?"

Worried with how she might sound if she tried to speak, Isabel just nodded and made her way over to a picnic table on the far end of the lawn. She settled in just as Jackson pulled a Sprite from the cooler and headed in her direction.

He kept his gaze turned down toward the ground, allowing Isabel some time to study him. And then the thought of Bobby entered her mind.

If given the same opportunity, would Bobby know what

to get her? Would he know what she liked and didn't like? And if the answer to those questions was no, why did that make her so sad?

Before she could settle on an answer, Jackson set the plate down in front of her and handed her the soda and a fork. He stood there awkwardly, as if trying to decide what he was going to do.

"Sit," she said, nodding toward the spot next to her.

She could feel his hesitation before he dropped down onto the bench. He must have misjudged the space between them, because as he sat, their legs brushed one another.

Warmth spread across her skin as she reveled in his touch.

There was something about Jackson. There always had been. He was familiar, and he knew her like she knew him. She would be lying if she didn't admit that that familiarity was something she missed. Wholly and completely.

Not sure what to say, Isabel shoved her fork into the potato salad and took a bite. Jackson seemed to be just as confused. He sat there with his hands on his knees, staring hard at the tabletop in front of them.

Feeling sad that this was what they'd come to, Isabel let out a soft sigh and turned to focus on Jackson. "Are you going to eat?" she asked.

Jackson startled and glanced over at her. He held her gaze for a moment and then shook his head. "I'm not hungry."

Isabel nodded as she slipped a chip into her mouth.

Silence engulfed them like fog on an autumn morning. She hated it. Hated how awkward things were between them.

"Are you excited for the wedding?" she asked, desperate to talk about something. Anything.

Jackson scoffed as he rested his hands on the tabletop. Then he hesitated before he glanced over at her. "You mean Jonathan's?"

Isabel nodded. "Who else would I be talking about?"

Jackson stared at her and then dropped his gaze down to the ring on her finger.

Realization hit her as she fiddled with the band. Right. Her wedding. Or lack thereof. She still wasn't sure what was going to happen with that.

Jackson cleared his throat as he shifted on his seat. "Yeah, I'm excited for Jonathan. He and Tiffany are perfect for each other. I'm happy that they're happy."

Isabel nodded as she felt a soft smile form on her lips. If only her own love life was that simple. To love someone and have them love her back. That felt like the perfect ending to her story.

And yet, that tale felt as far away as Bobby did.

"Is there someone for you like that? You know..." Isabel swallowed as heat crept across her skin. Why was she asking this? Did she really want to know? Judging by the rock that had just sunk in her stomach, she didn't. But she'd already started down the path, she might as well finish it. "...back in New York."

Jackson's gaze drifted over to her as he studied her in

silence. She pinched her lips, wondering if she'd made a big mistake. It wasn't an unusual question to ask an ex. People were normally curious about what the other person had been up to.

Jackson drummed his fingers on the tabletop and sighed. "No one in particular comes to mind. I've been busy. Not many women are okay with my work schedule."

Isabel took another bite of her potato salad as she studied her plate. "Your work is really important to you, isn't it?" she asked.

Jackson nodded. "It's my life. I've worked hard and made something of myself." The last few words were lower than the others. Almost like he was trying to prove something to himself. Or to her. But why would he need to prove anything to her? She'd never questioned his ability to be successful.

He had been valedictorian in high school. When Jackson Braxton put his mind to something, he accomplished it.

She gave him an encouraging smile. "I knew you would. I don't think anyone here in Honey Grove doubted you."

Jackson's gaze rose to meet hers. He looked surprised. Like he didn't believe her. Which was silly—there wasn't one person she knew who hadn't thought Jackson would make something of himself. When he wanted something, he stopped at nothing to get it.

And when he wanted something, it didn't matter who he hurt to get it.

Realizing that her throat was tightening up, Isabel took a swig of her Sprite and calmed her mind. That wasn't why she was there. She needed to focus on eating, and then she could fake exhaustion and head home.

"How's your dad?" Jackson asked, glancing over at her.

Isabel shrugged. Talking about her dad wasn't going to help with her nerves either. But, it did take her mind off the feelings for Jackson that nagged at the back of her mind. "He's okay, I guess. I haven't visited him in a few days. He's losing his memories. It's getting harder each time I go. But"—Isabel reached out to fiddle with her can—"I can't leave him. He's done so much for me. I just wish I could get him out of that home."

The feeling of failure hit her like a train. She knew in her mind she was failing, but speaking the words out loud killed her. She blinked back tears as she took another drink, hoping it would calm her down.

It didn't.

Grabbing a napkin, she dabbed her eyes. Why did she keep breaking down?

She was sick of being a mess. She was sick and tired of all of this. But she couldn't see the light at the end of the tunnel. She just felt lost.

"Getting your dad back into your house means that much to you?" Jackson's voice was low, and when she glanced over to focus on him, she saw that his eyebrows were drawn together.

His familiar blue eyes were soft and so familiar that it

made her soul ache. Jackson, for so long, had felt untouchable. But he was here right now, and in this moment he was all that existed.

It was getting harder to convince her heart not to fall, fast and hard, for Jackson Braxton.

"Yes," she whispered, allowing her gaze to drop down to Jackson's lips. Then, feeling like an idiot, she returned her gaze to his eyes.

"Jackson, there you are!" A loud, high-pitched voice filled the air, grabbing Jackson's attention.

Isabel looked too, only to see Tori Hodges sauntering over to them. She was wearing a miniskirt and cropped tank. Her heels kept sinking into the sod, and she had to balance on her tiptoes to keep her shoes on.

Not sure what was going on, Isabel glanced over at Jackson. He looked startled, but not surprised. Had he invited Tori?

Feeling like an idiot, Isabel grabbed her purse and scrambled to stand. "I should go," she said as she moved to grab her plate. Jackson beat her to it, grasping it with both hands.

"Stay. Finish," he said as he stood and motioned for Tori to follow him.

Not sure what to do, Isabel sat there, staring at her remaining food. She couldn't help but feel completely out of place.

Jackson's date showing up only solidified what she already knew—her relationship with the Braxtons was over and had been for a long time. It had been foolish of her to come.

She should have stayed home in the protection of her house where she was focused on the only thing that mattered to her—getting married so her father could walk her down the aisle and getting him home.

Desperate to get out of there, Isabel shoveled the rest of the food into her mouth. She could see Jackson and Tori talking to each other from the corner of her eye, and she didn't want to see what the rest of the evening was going to bring.

She was tired and ready to get the heck out of this place.

So when Mr. Braxton started up the music and the party goers all cheered, Isabel took that as her sign to leave. Grabbing her purse, she made her way over to the garbage, threw her plate away, and clung to the shadows as she headed to the front of the house.

There was a moment, before she disappeared from sight, that she thought she heard someone call her name, but she just continued on to her car and climbed inside.

She drove home in silence, holding her emotions in until she was in her pajamas and crawling into bed.

Once she was in the safety of her comforter, she let her tears flow.

On the one hand, it was good that Jackson had asked Tori to come. It helped solidify just how done they were. And it was good that she went to the Braxton dinner. Hopefully, Mrs. Braxton now saw that she and Jackson was over and that her matchmaking efforts would be for naught.

It was time for everyone to accept that nothing was going to happen between Jackson and her.

Ever.

FOURTEEN

JACKSON

JACKSON WAS STARING AT TORI, trying to pay attention to what she was saying. But his mind kept wandering. He couldn't help but think about Isabel and their conversation at the table. Right now, all he wanted to do was find a way to get Tori to leave.

He really wasn't sure why he'd asked her to come, and now she was the last person he wanted to see. He needed to let her down gently. He had been trying to fill a void with her, and it wasn't fair. Leading her on wasn't one of his proudest moments.

He'd been nothing but a jerk to everyone this whole weekend. He'd focused entirely on himself and the pain that seemed to take over his entire body. That wasn't the type of guy he was. He could be better than that. He would be better than that.

"So, this is what goes on at a famous Jackson Braxton

party," Tori said, leaning into him and giving him a seductive smile.

Jackson glanced around, confused about what she was talking about, and then realization hit him. Back in high school, Jackson had been known to throw some major parties. "Yeah, they've definitely mellowed out since senior year."

Tori snorted as she waved toward his parents, who were playing a card game. "I'd say so." She adjusted her skirt and turned to glance up at him. "It's okay. I know of a great place with booze and music. Wanna come?" Tori wrapped her arm around his.

Jackson dropped his gaze as she inched even closer to him. Heat pricked his skin as he glanced back to the picnic table and saw that Isabel had left. Confused, he scanned the backyard only to come up empty-handed. She was gone. Had slipped out when he wasn't looking.

Frustration coursed through him as he stepped away from Tori. "I don't think so. I haven't really spent that much time around my family. I should stay here."

Tori's nose wrinkled as she stared at Jackson. Then she let out a long and annoyed sigh. "Well, I didn't get this dressed up just to sit in someone's backyard."

Jackson nodded. "Yeah. I don't think there's going to be much partying around here."

Tori folded her arms as she tapped her fingers against her skin. "I think I'm going to go," she said.

Jackson shoved his hands into his front pockets. "If you think it's best."

Tori glanced over at him. "It's a real bummer. I've always wanted to go out with the famous Jackson Braxton."

Jackson laughed, thinking about his days as a teenager. There wasn't a lot that would have held him down back then. "Yeah, well, those days are long behind me."

"Clearly." Tori swept her gaze around again. "Well, I'm out of here." She reached up and patted his cheek with her hand. "If you ever want to have a good time, call me."

"Of course."

Tori gave him one last smile before she turned and headed toward the driveway. Once she was gone, Jackson walked over to the chair next to his mom and collapsed on it. He groaned as he closed his eyes and tipped his face toward the sky.

What an exhausting evening.

"Well, that was interesting," Sondra said, drawing his attention.

Jackson glanced over to see her staring at him. Whatever game his parents had been playing, they were done. Jimmy had his head tipped back, and a soft snore escaped his lips. Sondra, on the other hand, looked very much awake and very interested in talking to him.

And for the first time in a long time, Jackson actually wanted to talk to his mom about his problems. He was so confused, and it was resulting in him making dumb decisions. Right now, it was probably best to allow his mom to make his decisions for him.

"Tori was here, because...?" she asked, leaning toward him.

Jackson shrugged. "I accidentally threw sand on her at the beach. One thing led to another, and I invited her to dinner."

Sondra raised her eyebrows, and as Jackson's words settled in around him, he realized how juvenile he sounded. "I don't know what to do anymore, Ma," he said, scrubbing his face with his hands.

Sondra clicked her tongue. "Oh, Jackson, you're more lost than I thought." She reached down to grab her water bottle and took a swig. "Tori is not the girl for you."

Jackson nodded. That was the truth. "Yeah."

But neither was the girl he'd thought was his soul mate. How could she be? She was engaged. Destined to marry someone else. He should have moved on, but every effort he made ended in failure.

Sondra sighed, and Jackson turned to study her. He could see the thoughts floating around in her mind as she met his gaze. Leave it to his mother to have a solution for every problem her children faced.

"This is about Isabel, isn't it," Sondra said, slowly.

Jackson nodded. His mom was observant. As always.

"Because she's engaged."

Jackson nodded again, this time slower. It was painful,

thinking about Isabel with another man. It was painful to think about Isabel at all.

"What happened? When you called things off after high school—why did you just leave?"

Jackson leaned back in the lawn chair and rested his hands on his thighs. He swallowed, hard, thinking about his conversation with Isabel's dad. How he'd said Jackson wasn't worthy of his daughter. How Isabel's father had thought so little of him. It was a painful memory that he didn't want to relive.

But Sondra look expectant, so Jackson told her the story. By the time he was finished, Sondra's lips were parted, and fury radiated from her eyes. "My son? Dirk Andrews said that about my son?"

Jackson shrugged. There was a small part of him that was relieved his mother was angry that someone would say that about him. That, perhaps, he *was* worthy of Isabel's affection.

Sondra pinched her lips together as she tried to calm herself down. A few seconds passed before she spoke again. "Isabel never said these things to you?"

Jackson sighed as he shook his head. "No."

"And she doesn't believe that about you?"

Jackson shrugged. He wanted to believe that it had only been Mr. Andrews, but he could be wrong.

"Jackson, I've seen the way Isabel looks at you. There's no way she felt that way about you. Or that she feels that way now." Sondra grew quiet. "You left because you didn't want to make her choose between you and her father. Right?"

A twinge started in Jackson's throat as he mulled over his mom's words. Maybe there was some truth in that. He'd been afraid that if he told Isabel what her father had said, she would admit she felt the same. So, in an act of self-preservation, he'd responded first. He'd walked away while the pain still felt bearable.

Sondra wrapped her hand around his and squeezed. "Mr. Andrews is an idiot. You are wonderful."

Jackson cleared his throat. He loved his mom, but he still wasn't in the mood to get that sappy. "Thanks, Ma," he said, smiling over at her.

She studied him for a moment before pulling her hand back and tapping her chin with her forefinger. "Now, let's focus on what can be done."

Jackson furrowed his brow. "About what?"

Sondra tipped her head to the side. "This"—she waved around the backyard—"is not you. My son is loyal to a fault, so inviting another girl over when his ex is here is an act of desperation, not malice. You've sent out your distress signal, and now I'm here to help."

It amazed him that even though it'd been years since he'd come home, his mom still knew him. She knew what he needed. He wasn't the kind of guy who used women like what he'd done with Tori. He knew spending time with her wouldn't fill the gaping hole inside of his chest.

"What would make you happy?" Sondra asked, bending down to catch his gaze.

Jackson glanced at her and shrugged. "Seeing Isabel happy. Whatever it takes."

Sondra clapped her hands together. "Then that's what we'll do." She laughed, startling Jimmy awake.

Jimmy reached over and engulfed her hands with his. "What are you going on about, woman?" he boomed in a loving voice.

"I'm fixing Jackson's love life."

Jimmy glanced over at Jackson, who just shrugged.

"I've been doing a poor job of it so far," Jackson admitted. "Thought I'd give Mom a shot."

Jimmy chuckled as he reached down and grabbed his beer. "Do you know what you're saying, son? Once your mother gets cooking, it's hard to get her out of the kitchen."

Jackson chuckled. "Yeah. But this time, I think I'm okay with it."

"What's going on?" James asked as he, Jonathan, and Josh made their way over.

"Jackson is fixing his love life," Sondra said in a matter-of-fact tone.

Jackson winced. It was one thing to have his parents involved. It was a whole other thing to involve his siblings.

"With Isabel?" Josh asked.

Jackson nodded.

"What's the plan?" Jonathan asked.

"What are we planning?" Beth appeared behind Josh,

wrapping her arm around his waist and pulling herself in close.

"We're fixing Jackson's love life."

"Ooo," Layla said as she waddled over and rested her back against James. "I love this idea."

Jackson glanced around at his brothers, their wives, and his parents. Even Jenna walked up and gave him a wink.

"If it makes Jackson happy," Jenna said, "I'm all for it."

Jackson smiled. He'd felt so alone since he got to Honey Grove, but now, with his family all around him, he felt at home. He wasn't sure what was going to happen or how things would work out, but he knew that being true to himself was going to bring him the greatest joy.

"So what's the plan?" Dean asked, rubbing his hands together.

Jackson glanced over at his brothers. "Isabel wants her dad home, and I'm thinking we can make that happen." He ran his hands through his hair as thoughts started swarming around in his mind. "If all of us work together, we can outfit her home to better suit her dad's needs."

Jimmy clapped his hands. "With my boys all home, it'll be easy."

Jackson glanced up at Tiffany, hesitating to see what she thought. After all, this was her wedding weekend.

Tiffany had a huge smile on her face. "Jonathan and I have a few things to take care of tomorrow morning, and then you can count on us for the rest of the day."

Jackson smiled at his future sister-in-law. His brother had made the right choice. She was perfect.

"Thanks, Tiff," he said, winking at her.

She grinned back. "Anything to help Isabel. Besides, you'll need some of this raw muscle power to get the work done." She moved to squeeze Jonathan's arm but then flexed her own muscles, kissing her biceps for effect.

Laughter erupted around the group.

"Tomorrow, eight a.m. sharp, we'll head over to the Andrews' residence and get started," Jimmy said as he stood and gathered his trash. "I'm headed to bed."

They all said good night to Jimmy and Sondra as they walked back to the house, hand in hand. Jackson watched his parents, a dull ache forming in his chest. That was what he wanted. A love to last a lifetime.

His parents didn't always have a perfect marriage. He remembered his dad spending time on the couch after a fight with his mom, but they always got through it. They always found a way to fight for their future.

That was what he wanted to do. He wanted to fight for Isabel. Even if it meant she stayed with Bobby. Jackson needed to know he'd done everything he could to make her life a happy one. 'Cause she deserved that happiness.

After his brothers and their significant others had said their goodbyes, Jackson headed up the stairs to the small apartment over the garage. So many thoughts and plans were swarming in his mind, and he was ready to tackle them all.

His family was going to help get Isabel's house ready, but there was so much more that needed to get done. An in-home nurse came to mind. Someone to watch after Mr. Andrews when Isabel couldn't be there.

That was something he could do. A good use of the money he'd earned for himself.

Grabbing his phone, he called Journey, his assistant. As it rang, he started jotting down a list of things he needed to do. Journey answered. She was sleepy but happy to hear from him.

"I've got a job for you," Jackson said as he leaned back in his chair, staring at the list in front of him.

"Oh yeah?" Journey asked.

"Yep. Get a pen and paper, we've got things to do."

FIFTEEN

ISABEL

ISABEL FLIPPED from one side to the other, pinching her eyes shut. No amount of hope was helping sleep come to her.

Groaning, she flipped to her back and let out a very unhappy harrumph. It was two in the morning, and she hadn't slept a wink. Instead, she spent the entire night tossing and turning. It felt as if a brick had taken up residence in her stomach.

Her mind was swirling with thoughts of Jackson. Of Bobby. Of Dad.

And they weren't helpful thoughts either. All she could think about was how she was letting down everyone in her life.

She couldn't manage to be a good friend, daughter, or fiancée. It seemed like she was failing in every relationship she had. Epically.

Tired of trying to force sleep, she pulled off the covers and padded into the bathroom. She turned on the faucet and let the water run over her fingers. The cool temperature shocked her body and magically relaxed her.

After filling a glass and drinking the whole thing, she turned the water off and set the glass down on the counter. She made her way back into her bed, where she clicked on the side-table lamp and grabbed her phone.

She snuggled into the blankets and pillows as she swiped her screen on and opened her photos app.

After a few swipes, she found a video she'd taken last summer. Dad and Bobby were front and center, and she was holding the phone. They were telling her dad that they were engaged.

Dad had the biggest smile on his face as he glanced back and forth between them.

"Are you serious?" he asked, his deep voice booming.

"Yes," Isabel's voice squeaked with excitement.

"We're getting married!" Bobby exclaimed as Isabel's hand came into view. He kissed her fingers and Isabel giggled.

"I'm the luckiest man alive," her dad said, reaching forward and pulling her into a hug. The camera was smushed against his shirt and there was a scratching noise as the material brushed against the microphone.

He held her for a moment before he pulled back with tears in his eyes.

"You've made me the happiest dad in the world." His

hand disappeared, but Isabel knew what he was doing. He was wiping her tears away.

"Thanks, Dad," Isabel said.

"And maybe soon, some grandkids?" her dad asked, raising his eyebrows.

"Dad! One thing at a time."

Her dad's gaze intensified as he stared at the camera. "I want to see some babies before it's my time."

There was some silence before Bobby clapped her dad on the shoulder and changed the subject.

Isabel stared at the screen as she pulled up the covers. She paused the video on her father, tears welling up in her eyes.

This was what her father wanted. This was what was going to make him happy. This was why she couldn't give up on Bobby.

If she could give him just a sliver of happiness, she was going to.

Her dad deserved it.

Exhaustion took over, and before Isabel knew it, her eyes drifted closed and her body began to relax. Sleep was just within her grasp, but not before she made a promise to her dad all over again.

She was going to do the one thing that would make her father proud of her. She was going to show him that even when he was gone, she would be taken care of.

And Bobby was the person to do that.

ISABEL WOKE up the next morning to the sharp sound of someone knocking on her door. She blinked a few times as she stared up at the ceiling, waiting for the sound to come again.

Knock, knock, knock.

Great. So it hadn't been her imagination.

Sighing, she pulled off the covers and slipped her feet onto the floor. After grabbing her robe and pulling it around her body, she padded down the stairs and over to the front door. She peeked through the sidelight.

Jimmy Braxton was standing there with James, Josh, and Jackson behind him. They were talking and laughing with each other.

Completely confused, Isabel unlocked the bolt and pulled open the door. "Yes?" she asked, squinting against the bright morning light.

Jimmy grinned down at her. "We're here to help," he said.

Isabel furrowed her brow. "I'm sorry, what?"

"You want to get your dad home, we're here to do that." He waved her to the side as he stepped into her house. After slipping off his shoes, he made his way into the living room with his tape measure.

Josh and James followed after him. Josh had a clipboard and pen and jotted down the measurements that Jimmy rattled off.

Jackson lingered by the door, leaning his shoulder against the doorjamb. "Hey," he said, offering her a soft smile.

She stared at him. "What's going on?"

Jackson ran his hands through his hair as he dropped his gaze to the ground and then looked back up at her. "We're here to help you get your dad back home. Dad's going to outfit your house with a ramp and fix any hazards he sees around the house. You know, so your dad can get around better in a wheelchair." He shifted his body until his back was resting on the frame. His hands were shoved into his front pockets as he studied her.

"Why?" she asked, emotion choking her throat.

Jackson's brows furrowed as he met her gaze. "You need help, and we can help." He gave her a soft smile. "We're friends, after all. Isn't that what friends do?"

Isabel blinked a few times, hoping to dispel the tears that were threatening to spill. "But..."

Jackson cleared his throat and straightened. "Isabel, you're important to our family, and we help family." He reached out and rested his hand on her shoulder. Warmth emanated from his touch and caused butterflies to erupt inside of her. "We're here for you."

Too scared to meet his gaze, all Isabel could do was nod. It had been a long time since anyone had cared for her like the Braxtons were doing right now. She felt safe and taken care of—something that Bobby never managed to do for her.

"Can I pay you?" she whispered.

Jackson shook his head. "Nope. It's on the house."

"Knock knock," Beth's soft voice said from behind Jackson. Isabel glanced back to see Beth's wide smile. "Hey, Isabel." She waved to Tiffany and Layla, who were standing behind her. "We're here to help as well."

Isabel nodded as she stepped back to let them in. Jenna made up the rear, and as she neared, she pulled Isabel into a one-armed hug.

Not sure how to take all of this kindness, Isabel just stood there. It was almost scary, opening herself up to these people. She didn't feel as if she deserved any of it.

"We're here—might as well put us to work," Layla said, raising the garbage bags in her hands. "We are here to help declutter and tidy up."

Isabel nodded as tears formed on her lids. She'd always wanted to update her dad's house but never had the time nor the knowledge to do it. The fact that these people—people who weren't even her family—had taken this upon themselves... Well, she wasn't sure how she was ever going to repay them.

———

IT WAS AMAZING how fast time went by when there were many hands to help. By late evening, Isabel's house was cleaned out of all unnecessary or outdated items. And Beth and Layla had written up a list of furniture for her to get that would help liven up the house.

Tiffany, Isabel, and Jenna spent the day painting and laughing as they gave the walls a facelift.

The guys spent a lot of the day outside, breaking down her crumbling front porch and replacing it with a ramp. They also added a ramp to the back door. Then they moved inside and took down any unnecessary walls that would impede her father's mobility when he got home.

Isabel couldn't help the tears that slid down her cheeks as she stood back and surveyed the work. Most of the helpers had left, declaring they were headed to get drinks and dinner at the local diner. Isabel wanted to go, too, but figured she should stay back.

They'd already helped her enough. There was no need to force herself into their family time.

"What do you think?" Jackson asked from behind her.

Startled, Isabel turned to see him standing there with his hands in his pockets. There was a dirt smudge across his face that made him look even more adorable than she'd thought possible.

She shook her head slightly, forcing those thoughts from her mind. Jackson wasn't hers. For all she knew, Tori and Jackson had hit it off last night and were now an item.

His helping her with her house was just one friend helping out another. Hadn't that been what he said?

This meant nothing, romantically speaking.

"Thanks," she whispered as she wiped at a tear. "I mean it. You didn't have to do any of this."

Jackson studied her. "Yes, I did."

Isabel scoffed. "Why?"

Jackson blew out his breath and pushed his hands through his hair. "Because I care about you, Isabel."

His words surrounded her, warming her skin. Her heart picked up speed. What did that mean? "You do?"

Jackson held her gaze and then blew out his breath as he turned to look at her house. "I ran away back then, and I shouldn't have. I was too scared about what you would say if you found out..." His voice drifted off as he nudged the ground with his toe.

Confused, Isabel stared at him. "Found out what?"

Jackson's jaw was clenched as he studied his feet. He looked as if he wasn't sure what he should say.

"Jackson," Isabel said, reaching out and resting her hand on his forearm. His skin was warm under her fingertips and sent jolts of electricity through her body.

There was a familiarity in touching him, and she couldn't imagine ever letting go.

Jackson's gaze made its way over to her hand. Then he sighed and glanced up at her. "Never mind. It's in the past. What happened, happened." He gave her a soft smile. "I'm just happy I was able to help you with this." He turned to face her, effectively breaking their connection. "You deserve to be happy."

She studied him as his words washed over her. He was right. Happiness was what she was searching for, but right now, she wasn't sure that she was actually accomplishing that goal.

There was nothing about marrying Bobby and moving halfway across the world that was going to bring her happiness. Leaving Honey Grove was the last thing she wanted to do, and being with Jackson was helping her realize that. If she did want that complete joy she was looking for, being with Bobby wasn't going to bring that.

"Thank you," she whispered as she glanced up at Jackson.

He furrowed his brow. "For what?"

She genuinely smiled for the first time in a long time. "For helping me see just what I needed."

He cleared his throat. "And what was that?"

She studied him and then moved her gaze over to her house. "Happiness."

When Jackson didn't respond, she glanced at him to see that he was staring down at her. There was desire in his gaze. And it caused her heart to pound harder in her chest.

"Good. You deserve it." His voice had dropped an octave now. It was warm and intense. It was filled with so many memories and emotions that Isabel wasn't sure if she could breathe.

"Jackson, I—" The sound of a car pulling into the driveway behind her drew her attention. Staring at the yellow taxi, Isabel tried to figure out who it could be.

It wasn't until Bobby's six-foot frame climbed out of the backseat that she realized who it was. Her heart pounded harder as she glanced over at Jackson and then back to Bobby.

"Hey, baby," Bobby said as he dropped his suitcase and rushed over to her, wrapping both arms around her and pulling her close. He pressed his lips to hers and held them there for a moment.

Feeling uncomfortable with kissing in front of Jackson, Isabel pulled back and stepped away from Bobby, who growled his protest. Isabel chewed her bottom lip as she glanced over at Jackson. He was staring hard at the ground in front of him.

Bobby extended his hand toward Jackson. "Bobby Johnson," he said, introducing himself.

Jackson glanced up at Bobby and then met his handshake. "Jackson," he muttered.

"Jackson? Like, *the* Jackson?" Bobby asked as he glanced over at Isabel.

There had been a few times Isabel had mentioned Jackson to Bobby, but she didn't realize he'd actually heard her. Apparently, he had.

"Yeah. His family was just here. They helped me upgrade the house so Dad can come home," she said.

Bobby glanced at the house and then back over to Jackson. "That's nice of them. You could have waited until I got back," he said as he wrapped his arm around Isabel's waist and pulled her close.

Shock took over her body as she stared at Bobby. "You were on your way to Australia," she said, hoping that she could hide the hurt in her voice.

Bobby chuckled. "That was before I missed my girl and

had to come back." He turned her hips until she was facing him. Then he leaned down, resting his forehead on hers. "Let's get married this weekend," he murmured.

It sounded as if he were trying to be romantic, but right now, it was just irritating. "What?"

Bobby pressed his lips to her cheek. "I want to marry you right now. Let's get your dad and find a justice of the peace."

Isabel pushed against his chest as she stepped back.

"I think I'm going to go," Jackson said.

Isabel turned to see that he was already halfway down the yard. She wanted to call after him. To tell him not to go, but she couldn't find the right words to get him to stay.

"See ya," Bobby said, waving Jackson away.

Isabel studied Jackson as he made his way to his car. She hoped he'd turn around to say goodbye, but he didn't. Instead, he climbed into his car and drove away, not once meeting her gaze.

Feeling defeated, she glanced back at Bobby, who had a smug look on his face. He dropped his hand and entwined it with hers. "I missed you," he said.

Isabel studied him, wanting to say the same thing, but she couldn't get the words out. Had she missed Bobby?

Maybe.

Or maybe she'd just missed the thought of him. He was the representation of everything she'd thought she wanted. Someone to care for her so she didn't feel alone anymore. A wedding. Someone her father approved of.

But now she wasn't sure that he was the right person to fill that void.

"Why are you here?" she asked, allowing him to guide her up the brand-new ramp and into the house.

Bobby shut the door behind them. Turning, he wrapped his hands around her waist and pulled her close. "I missed you. I thought about what you said, and I don't want to be without you again."

Isabel studied him as she tried to read his intentions. Then she stepped out of his arms and made her way into the living room to sit on one of the only chairs left from Beth and Layla's purge.

"What happened to all of your furniture?" Bobby asked.

Isabel pulled her knees to her chest and hugged them. "I'm trying to start over. The Braxtons are helping me."

Bobby stared at her for a moment before he huffed and took a seat next to her. "What about me? I can take care of you. Help you."

Isabel stared at him. "You? You've been gone for months. I've been doing everything by myself."

Bobby ran his hands through his hair as he glanced around. "But I'm here now."

Isabel tipped her head back on the chair and closed her eyes. She allowed her breath to escape as she nodded. "True."

"And I want to marry you. Did that Jackson guy want to marry you?"

Isabel swallowed at Bobby's question. Once, she'd

thought he wanted to marry her. But that had all changed when Jackson ran away.

Maybe she was a fool to think that things had changed between them. After all, Jackson did say that he was helping her as a friend. And friends don't marry each other.

Maybe Jackson felt bad for abandoning her. Maybe he felt bad that her life had spiraled out of control. That she was alone when he had this great big family to take care of him.

And why would she put her trust in Jackson? After all, if she left Bobby and Jackson decided that he wanted nothing to do with her, she would be right back where she'd been before.

Alone.

And that was a risk she wasn't sure she was willing to take. Or could take. Not when her heart was squeezing itself in two.

"You want to get married this weekend?" she asked, straightening her head to glance at Bobby.

He'd moved to the far wall and had his hands shoved into his pockets. "Yes," he said.

Isabel shifted in her seat and stood. "Good. 'Cause I want to get married as well."

Bobby whooped and wrapped his arms around her, pulling her close. He pressed his lips to hers, and Isabel tried to force her feelings for him to surface.

It was probably just because he'd been gone for a long

time. After all, they hadn't seen each other in a while, maybe they just needed to get back into a groove.

When Bobby pulled away, he didn't act as if there had been anything different about the kiss. Instead, he smiled down at her. "I have a surprise for you."

Isabel studied him, a smile emerging on her lips. Maybe she had been wrong. Sure, Bobby had been gone for a while, but him showing up to marry her early and arranging a surprise, on top of paying to fix her car, made her think that maybe she'd read everything wrong.

"Really?" she asked.

Bobby nodded. "It's coming tomorrow, so you'll have to wait until then."

Isabel nodded, forcing down the nervous feeling inside of her. She was going to be okay. She was.

This was what she wanted.

Right?

SIXTEEN

JACKSON

JACKSON'S STOMACH was in knots as he drove down the street and away from Isabel's home. Every emotion from sadness to rage was coursing through him at that very moment.

It was taking all of his strength not to turn his car around and face Bobby What's-his-name head on. He wanted to tell him off. To ask him why he would just leave Isabel alone the way he had. Or why he had shown up unexpectedly and demanded that they get married right away.

Where had he been while Isabel was going through the pain of watching her father slip away? Why hadn't he been there for her, taking care of her like a fiancé should do?

Jackson gripped the steering wheel and pressed on the breaks as the light ahead of him flipped from yellow to red. He wanted to blow through the light and take off down the road, leaving his troubles in the dust. But he knew that would inevitably lead to a traffic ticket, and that would only push his already sour mood over the top.

Besides, he wasn't even sure running away would make him feel any better. Even if he left tonight, he'd just be right back here in Honey Grove for Jonathan and Tiffany's wedding.

No matter how much he wanted to go, he would stay.

So he flipped on his blinker, and when the light turned green, he took a left toward his parents' house.

It wasn't long before he pulled into the driveway and killed the engine. He took a moment to gather his thoughts as he scrubbed his face and pushed his hands through his hair.

He wasn't sure what he'd expected from Isabel when he got there that morning to help outfit her house, but watching her recommit to her fiancé hadn't even entered his mind.

Perhaps, he'd hoped she would see him showing up as some grand gesture. That she would see he'd changed. That she would see what he'd known all along.

They were perfect for each other.

But that didn't happen.

Jackson let out a groan as he pulled on the door handle and climbed out of his car. After slamming the door a little too hard, he clenched his hands into fists. None of that made him feel any better. If anything, it made him feel worse.

No amount of anger was going to bring Isabel back to him. She was Bobby's fiancée, and after this weekend, she would be his forever.

"You okay, sweetie?" Sondra's voice drifted from the porch.

Jackson waved his hand in his mom's direction as he kept his head down and quickened his pace toward the garage.

"Excuse me, young man," Sondra said in a tone that made Jackson stop in his tracks.

He knew that voice.

"Sorry, Ma," he said, turning and heading to where she stood. She had her hands on her hips and a concerned look in her eye.

"Get up here and have some cookies and milk with your mother," she said, pointing her finger down next to her.

Jackson glanced up at her. He took deep breath in and then nodded. There was no use fighting her. Sondra Braxton got what Sondra Braxton wanted. She always did.

"Okay," he said, making his way around to the porch steps. After he climbed them, he walked over to where she stood.

She glanced up at him for a moment, as if she could read him like a book, and then wrapped her arm around his and led him toward the back door. Jackson twisted the handle and held the door for his mom, following in after her.

Once they were in the kitchen, Sondra waved him toward the table. He watched as his mom busied herself grabbing the milk jug and glasses in one arm and the cookie jar in the other.

Wanting to help his mom, Jackson stood, pulled out the

chair next to him, and then helped her unload the food and drink.

After the milk was poured and Sondra set a handful of cookies in front of Jackson, she settled back in her chair with an expectant look on her face.

Jackson picked up a cookie and dipped it into the milk as he tried to gather his thoughts. He knew his mom wanted answers, but he really wasn't sure how to give them.

"Best to start at the beginning," Sondra said in an encouraging voice.

Jackson took a bite of his cookie and nodded.

"Bobby's back," he said, figuring it was probably best to just cut to the chase.

"Who?"

Jackson shifted in his seat as he fiddled with the crumbs on the table. "Bobby. Isabel's fiancé."

When he glanced over at his mom, he saw that her eyebrows were raised, and she looked as surprised as he felt. "Really? When did he get back?"

Jackson took another bite of his milk-soaked cookie. "Just after everyone left. He came rolling up in a taxi right when..." He let his voice drift off as the memory of his conversation with Isabel replayed in his mind.

He had been ready to tell her everything. Tell her how he felt—how he'd always felt. Tell her about her dad. Tell her about how leaving her was the worst thing he'd ever done.

And there was a moment there when he thought that she might admit the same...until Bobby showed up.

"You were going to tell her that you love her," Sondra said, matter-of-factly.

Jackson closed his eyes for a moment as his mom's words washed over him.

Love.

Yes. That was the truth. He loved Isabel. Body and soul. And time didn't seem to change that. How could it? It had been eight years since he'd seen her. But all it took was a few days, a few hours, to fall back in love with her.

And now he was right back where he'd been eight years ago, but this time there were two men standing in his way instead of one.

The feeling of his mom's hand on his caused him to open his eyes. He glanced over to see her soft smile. It amazed him how just being around his mom helped calm him down. Like she was there for him, willing to shoulder this burden with him, and it helped.

"Did you tell her?" Sondra asked.

Jackson cleared his throat. "Tell her what?"

Sondra tsked. "Tell her that you love her."

Jackson thought back to their conversation. "Not exactly. I told her that I cared about her."

Sondra gave an exaggerated sigh. "Honey, you can't afford to play around. If you love someone, you tell them. Openly and honestly. You can't expect her to know how you are feeling if you don't tell her."

Jackson blinked a few times as fear crept up inside of him. "But..."

How could he tell his mom that he was scared? It might be ridiculous, but it was the truth. If he told Isabel he loved her, he wasn't sure what she was going to do with that information. He needed to protect himself.

Sondra sighed as she held his gaze. "She's not a mind reader, love. She needs to hear the words. If what I saw earlier today was any indication of how she feels, I'd say she never truly gave up on you either."

Jackson's heart squeezed at his mom's words. Was that true? He parted his lips to speak, but Sondra beat him to it.

"Listen, you both are in the business of protecting your hearts, I get that. But at some point, one of you is going to need to take the plunge and risk being vulnerable." She said it so simply that is startled Jackson.

One of them would need to be the first to take the risk. He drummed his fingers on the table as nervous energy built up inside of him. "But—"

"I know Isabel Andrews. She loves her father, but she also loves you. Whatever Dirk Andrews felt eight years ago doesn't matter anymore, and I'm pretty sure it never mattered to Isabel. You need to give her the chance to walk away, not take it from her by running away first." Sondra picked up a cookie, gave it a good dunk, and took a bite.

She seemed so relaxed. But Jackson felt like a jumble of nerves.

Jackson leaned back in his chair as he folded his arms,

his mom's words rolling around in his mind. If he were honest with himself, he knew what Sondra said was true. He had yet again taken away Isabel's ability to make a decision about their relationship.

Eight years ago, he'd left. The fear that Isabel would repeat her father's sentiments had dictated his decisions. He'd made the choice for the both of them. It had been selfish, an act of self-preservation.

And now he wanted to give her the chance to decide what she wanted, except that chance was gone. "Her fiancé is here, and they are moving up the wedding," Jackson said as he covered his hands with his face.

Sondra chuckled.

Confused, Jackson dropped his hands to stare at his mom.

She took another bite of cookie as her laughter lingered in the air. Then she brushed the crumbs off her fingertips and smiled at him. "Oh, my son. You have such little faith in your mother."

Jackson studied her as her words settled in around him.

When he didn't respond right away, she sighed and straightened. "I don't consider myself a meddler when it comes to my children's lives, but I would classify myself as an encourager. Sometimes, it takes an outsider to see exactly what a person needs." She waved to her body. "Outsider."

Jackson chuckled as he leaned forward with his elbows on the table. "What exactly do you have in mind?"

A slow, cryptic smile spread across her lips. "Just leave that to me. You focus on what you're going to say to Isabel."

Fifteen minutes later, Jackson gave his mom a hug and walked out through the back door and over to the garage apartment. He climbed the stairs, unlocked the door, and slipped inside.

Jenna was sitting on the couch in the living room. She was curled up with a blanket and pillow, and she looked... sad. There was a rerun playing on the TV, but she didn't really look like she was watching it.

Jackson plopped down on the chair next to the couch and let out a sigh. Jenna startled as if she hadn't noticed him coming in. She quickly swiped at her cheeks and cleared her throat.

Worried that there was something wrong, Jackson leaned forward. But his concern was met with Jenna's forced smile.

"How was your evening?" she asked, beating him to the punch.

The day's events rushed back to him, and Jackson flopped back in exhaustion. "Long. Confusing. Stressful." He leaned his head against the back of the chair, tipping his face toward the ceiling. He closed his eyes and relaxed.

"How did things go with Isabel once we left?"

"Her fiancé came back."

There was a pause. "*What?*"

Jackson met Jenna's gaze. "Yep. He wants to speed up the wedding. They're planning it for this weekend."

Jenna stared at him for a moment and then let out her breath. She pulled the blanket up around her as she snuggled in deep. "We should have just stayed away," she said softly.

Confused, Jackson studied her. "We?"

Jenna didn't meet his gaze as she returned her attention to the TV.

"Jenna, what is going on? Why are you so sad?" Worried about his sister, Jackson stood and joined her on the couch.

Jenna shifted away from him, wrapping her arms around her chest. "It's nothing. I'm just overwhelmed by being here."

He didn't believe her. Jackson leaned forward to catch her gaze. "You'd tell me, wouldn't you? If there was something wrong?"

Jenna kept her gaze glued to the screen, but Jackson could see the strain in her neck as she swallowed. Something was definitely up, but he could tell from her body language that he was the last person she was going to tell.

So he sighed and leaned back, bringing one foot up to rest on the coffee table in front of them. He watched the screen for a few minutes before he turned to study Jenna one more time.

He hated that his sister seemed so upset. And he hated that she wasn't going to tell him what was going on. It was strange for her to be so standoffish. They'd never been like that towards each other.

It was probably his fault. He'd promised to be her buffer

this weekend, and yet, he'd spent most of his time trying to sort out his feelings for Isabel.

"I'm sorry," he said.

Jenna furrowed her brow as she glanced over at him. "For what?"

He looked at her for a moment. Had he misread the situation? Then he shook his head. It didn't matter. He felt bad about ditching his sister, and he should apologize. "For abandoning you this weekend. I know I was supposed to be there for you, and I wasn't. I'm sorry."

Jenna held his gaze and then sighed. "I know. And I'm not mad about it. You had to do what you had to do. I get it." She turned her attention back to the TV.

Jackson stared at her, trying to figure out what was the matter. If she wasn't mad at him, why was she so upset? And then it dawned on him. He knew that look. He knew that feeling. She'd had her heart broken.

"Who's the guy?"

Jenna snapped her attention over to him. "What?" she asked, her voice rising an octave.

Yep, that confirmed his suspicions. He poked her in the side as he smiled. "You can tell me."

Jenna jerked away from him as she raised her hand. "There is no guy."

Jackson gave her a look. He didn't believe a word of it. "Really?"

Jenna scooted toward the other end of the couch as she

buried herself again in the pillows and blanket. "No. No guy."

There was no way that was true, but he'd let her say that if it made her feel better. "Okay," he said with a sarcastic tone. He leaned back on the couch and brought up his ankle to rest on his knee. Then he threaded his fingers together and laid them on his chest.

Still not satisfied with his conversation with Jenna, he glanced over at her. "If there *was* a guy and he hurt you, you know I'd never let him live it down, right?"

A protective surge rushed through his body as he studied his little sister.

Jenna didn't move to look at him. Instead, she just pinched her lips together and nodded. "I know," she said.

That was as far as they were going to get, so Jackson sighed and leaned his head back, closing his eyes. If Jenna wanted some privacy, he'd give it to her. After all, he hated it when people poked their noses into his stuff.

Besides, he needed to focus on exactly what he was going to do tomorrow and what he was going to say. He loved Isabel, and he was ready to tell her that, no matter what she said in return.

If she turned him down, it would crush him, but at least he would know he'd done what he could. And that was all he could expect from himself.

SEVENTEEN

ISABEL

THE NEXT MORNING, Isabel woke up with a knot in her stomach. She lay in her bed, staring up at the ceiling above her. Last night, after Bobby had spun into her life and asked if she wanted to get married this weekend, they relaxed and watched a movie.

Bobby fell asleep on the couch and Isabel tried in vain to wake him, but he was no doubt exhausted from the jet lag.

And Isabel wasn't too heartbroken. She liked her privacy, liked waking up alone in her own bed. Here, she could think. When Bobby was around, he had a tendency to take over every conversation and shift situations to benefit him.

Which she was normally okay with. After all, it was his take-charge personality that had attracted her in the first place. He could make decisions when she felt indecisive.

And that was exactly how she felt. Nothing about yesterday had made her feel like she was making the right decisions in any part of her life.

It was so nice to have the Braxtons show up to help with her house. A weight had been lifted off of her chest now that she was finally one step closer to bringing her dad home. And the fact that Jackson had initiated it...well, her whole soul swelled at the prospect of what that meant.

And there had been a moment last night when she thought he was going to finally open up and be honest with her. When he was going to confess his feelings for her—and she'd wanted to do the same. But it never happened.

Instead, he left her with Bobby, so she'd given the only rational answer she could have to his proposal. She'd said yes.

Feeling frustrated with herself, Isabel threw off the covers and set her feet on the ground. She took in a few deep breaths and then made her way toward the bathroom for a shower. Hot water sounded like heaven right then.

Fifteen minutes later, she emerged from the steam, wrapped in a towel. She padded over to her dresser and changed into a pair of cut-off shorts and a flowy top. She pulled her hair from the towel that was wrapped around it and studied herself in the mirror.

She looked tired and stressed—a typical look for her. Reaching up, she tugged at her eyes and scrubbed her face with her hands. The pit in her stomach still remained. It seemed as if there wasn't much that was going to ease the dread that filled her whole body.

The dread that she might be making the wrong choice.

Sighing, she tugged a brush through her hair and then applied some mascara and lip gloss. She braided her hair and pulled a few wisps loose to frame her face. After staring at her reflection, she sighed and shook her head.

What was she going to do? How was she going to follow through on the one thing that she thought she wanted? Getting married to please her father had seemed like a good idea...until Jackson came back.

She'd begun to doubt that she could replace love with responsibility. At least, not when her feelings for Jackson were back in full force.

But he didn't feel the same. At least, he wasn't ready to commit like she so desperately wanted him to. And his inaction had left her to try and figure out what she was supposed to do. Which part of her heart she was going to be true to? Her love for her father or her feelings for Jackson.

"Ugh," she whispered, hoping that would help silence the ache inside of her.

Maybe after some breakfast and coffee, she would feel better. She opened her bedroom door and padded down the stairs to the kitchen.

She half expected to see Jackson sitting at her table as he'd done a few days before. Instead, her kitchen was empty. The only sound she could hear was Bobby's loud snore coming from the living room.

She swallowed, hoping to push down her disappointment. She needed to accept that they were never going to be anything more than friends. They weren't meant for each other. They'd had their chance and they both needed to move on.

Grabbing her coffee pot, she slipped it under the faucet and turned the water on. She stood there, in a sort of trance, as the pot filled up. Then she busied herself with starting the machine.

She wasn't sure what she even had in the fridge for breakfast, so she grabbed a slice of bread and slipped it into the toaster. Just as the bread popped up, a deep voice filled the air.

"Darn it, you're already up."

Isabel yelped and turned to see Jackson standing in her kitchen with a white bag in one hand and a coffee carrier in the other. He looked so good in his dark blue T-shirt and jeans. He kept glancing up at her and then back down as if he was embarrassed to be there.

Isabel's heart picked up speed as she shifted her weight. This was not how she was supposed to be feeling for Jackson, and yet she couldn't help herself. The sight of him caused her heart to gallop.

Hoping to calm her nerves, she leaned against the counter and folded her arms. "Are you making a habit of this?" she asked, unable to hide the teasing in her voice.

Jackson studied her for a moment and then walked over and set the white bag and coffee on the countertop. "I was here yesterday. I saw the state of your groceries. I thought I'd pick up some breakfast and drop it off before you got up." Jackson rested his hands on the counter and tipped his face down. His shoulders rose, and she could see the stress emanating from him.

Not sure what to say, she rubbed her face. "That's really kind of you," she said.

Why wasn't loving someone easy? The feelings came naturally, of course, but everything else seemed so stressful. Every decision she made had consequences, and she wasn't sure if she was making the right ones at all.

She glanced at the coffee, and out of instinct, she picked one up. She raised her gaze to see Jackson standing a few inches away. The depth of his gaze as he stared down at her sent shivers across her skin.

"Thanks," she whispered as she clung to the coffee like it was a lifeline.

"Yeah," Jackson replied as he returned to the drink carrier and got a cup for himself.

They sipped their coffee in silence. Right before Isabel thought she would drown in the words they weren't saying, Jackson parted his lips.

"Where's Bobby?" he asked as he glanced around the room.

Isabel's gaze drifted to the living room. She could still hear his snores. "He's sleeping. Jet lag has been terrible for him."

Jackson's gaze followed hers, and he nodded. "I got you a croissant," he said as he opened the bag.

Isabel's stomach rumbled in response. "That sounds amazing," she said, taking the one that he handed over to her.

The crunchy, delicate texture and buttery flavor filled her mouth as she bit into it. It tasted amazing. She closed her eyes for a moment and took in a deep breath. There was definitely something to say about food melting stress away.

When she opened her eyes again, her gaze automatically found Jackson. He was leaning against the counter with his arms folded. His expression was intense as he studied her.

Heat pricked her skin as she dropped her gaze to the floor. Fear and worry creeped up inside of her. Why was he looking at her like that? What did it mean?

Too scared of what he could do to her heart, Isabel busied herself with finishing breakfast. She could tell he wanted to talk, but she wasn't sure if she could handle the conversation. If she opened the door to her feelings for Jackson, would he stick around? Or would he run like he did eight years ago?

She'd finally pieced her life together enough to feel as if she could move on, but Jackson coming in and shaking up her world could only put her right back where she'd been when he left.

Once her croissant was gone, she brushed her hands against each other and took a sip of her coffee. She turned to Jackson and gave him a smile. "Thanks so much," she said.

Jackson nodded as he slipped the remaining portion of his croissant into his mouth. Then he took a few sips of coffee and turned to set the cup down on the counter. His back was to her, so she took that time to take a few deep breaths and center her mind.

Whatever was going to happen, good or bad, she needed to be ready for it.

"Isabel," Jackson whispered.

The intensity with which he said her name caused shivers to rush across her skin. Her whole body heated at the depth in his voice. Her pulse quickened as she returned his gaze.

"Yes?" she asked.

He stared down at her and slowly moved closer. She could feel his body in front of her as he leaned in. It was amazing that, even though they weren't touching, she could feel him. Could breathe him in.

"I..." His voice trailed off as he held her gaze. He studied her, the intensity in his eyes taking her breath away.

"Coffee?" Bobby's clouded voice shattered the tension that filled the air.

Isabel jumped back and whipped her gaze over to Bobby. His eyes were hazy as he shuffled into the kitchen.

"Right here," Jackson said as he handed over the remaining coffee cup.

Bobby took it and tipped it to his lips. A few seconds later, he shuffled over to the table, where he pulled out a chair and collapsed onto it.

Bobby seemed too distracted with rubbing his shoulder and neck to realize what had almost happened between Isabel and Jackson.

And as she thought back to her interaction, she wasn't sure what *had* happened between them. It felt as if he were going to tell her something important.

What did he want to say?

Her heart stuttered as she glanced around the room. Jackson was busying himself on his phone, and Bobby had both elbows resting on the tabletop, propping up his drooping head.

"I should go," Jackson said after he slipped his phone into his pocket.

Isabel glanced up at him. Sadness crept into her soul as she instinctively stepped forward. "Are you sure?"

Jackson held her gaze for a moment and then nodded. "Yeah. I'll see myself out." He turned and made his way over to the back door. After the soft sound of the door closing, Isabel let out her breath.

"Why was he here?" Bobby mumbled.

Isabel made her way over to the sink to distract herself with the few dishes that were inside. Part of her wanted to run after Jackson. The other part of her worried what would happen if she did.

Would he take her back? Did he care about her that way? Was she willing to risk everything to find out?

Fear and pain coated her mind as she stared out the kitchen window to her backyard. She knew Bobby was talking to her, but she just couldn't pay attention to him. All she could think about was Jackson and how he was leaving. Again.

"I can't do this," she whispered, closing her eyes as she allowed her words to wash over her. She could be strong. She needed to do the right thing despite how scared she felt.

Nancy had been right. Her father would never want her to be unhappy, and being with Bobby would do just that.

"What?" Bobby's voice drew nearer.

She glanced over her shoulder to see that he was a few feet away from her. She sucked in her breath as she took in his confused expression.

Tears pricked her eyes, but she didn't allow them to fall. She was done with crying. She was done with feeling out of control. Her life was in her hands, and it was her job to make the most of it.

"I can't marry you, Bobby." She reached over to her left hand and pulled the ring off.

Bobby's gaze followed her movement, and his eyebrows rose higher as she reached over and placed the ring in his open hand.

"We want different things. I thought I could justify making exceptions because it would make me happy." She pinched her lips. "But I'm not happy, and I don't think you are either."

Bobby's gaze had dipped down to the ring that was nestled in his palm. He fiddled with it for a moment and then glanced back up at her. "Is that what you really want?"

Isabel pinched her lips together and nodded. "It's what I need to do. I want to stay in Honey Grove. You want to see the world. I just don't see how we can make that work."

Bobby stared at her for a moment before he nodded. "Yeah. It was a fool's errand to think we could pull that off." He sighed as he glanced around. "Well, I guess this is it then," he said, slipping the ring into his front pocket.

"I guess it is." Isabel hugged her chest. It felt as if her whole soul was breaking. Even though ending things with Bobby was a risk, she knew it was the right thing to do. Besides, her dad would understand. She knew he only wanted her happiness. And for the first time, she was going to think about herself and what she wanted first.

Bobby reached out and wrapped his arms around her. He held her for a moment before he pulled away. "You're a great girl, Isabel," he said as he pressed his lips to the top of her head.

Isabel smiled as she pulled back. "You're a great guy, and you'll find a girl who wants to go on all your adventures with you."

Bobby chuckled as he dropped his arms and shoved his hands into his front pockets. "Yeah. She's out there, right?"

Isabel nodded. "Of course."

Bobby glanced over at her and smiled. "And the same goes for you."

Isabel's just smiled softly at his words. Truth was, she'd already found the person she wanted to spend her life with.

He was the guy who'd wiggled his way into her heart a long time ago and had never really left.

Her only fear was that he didn't feel the same. But that was a risk she was willing to take.

From now on, she was determined to be happy. She'd spent too much of her life living for other people.

Not anymore.

EIGHTEEN

JACKSON

JACKSON PULLED INTO HIS PARENTS' driveway, frustration brewing in his stomach. He killed the engine and pulled the keys from the ignition. Then he sat there, with his hands on the wheel and his head tipped forward.

Why was he such a fool? Why had he thought things would change?

Did he really think that if he showed up at Isabel's with coffee and croissants, she would come running back to him? Was he that naive?

Apparently.

But even though he'd known going was a risk, he couldn't stop himself. He loved her. Wholly and completely. With every fiber of his being, he loved her. And he wanted to spend the rest of his life showing her that.

But it wasn't in the cards for him.

She had Bobby, and he had...no one.

Growling, he grabbed the handle and flung the car door open. He stepped out onto the asphalt and slammed the door shut behind him.

He was ready for his vacation to be over. He'd had as much Honey Grove as he could handle. The wedding tomorrow couldn't come soon enough.

Jackson made his way across the driveway, up the back steps, and into the kitchen. The smell of bacon and eggs filled his nose.

His stomach grumbled as he shut the door behind him and walked over to his mom, wrapping his arm around her shoulders. He kissed her on the top of her head.

"This smells delicious, Ma."

Sondra patted his arm as she shifted away from him so she could pull a waffle from the waffle maker. "Good. You need your strength up if you're going to talk to Isabel today."

Jackson sucked in his breath.

Sondra twisted her body around, shoving her finger in his direction. "What did you do?"

Jackson held up his hands. "I went to her house this morning."

Sondra narrowed her eyes. Then she sighed and folded her arms across her chest. "Why?"

Saying the words "I can't stay away" sounded pathetic, so Jackson just shrugged. "She didn't have food, so I brought her some breakfast." Jackson reached behind his mom and grabbed a slice of bacon.

Sondra studied him for a moment and then shrugged.

"Good." She swatted his shoulder. "But next time, stick to the plan."

Jackson swallowed hard, a sharp piece of bacon scraping his throat on the way down. He blinked a few times as tears from the pain filled his eyes. Then he cleared his throat and reached over to grab a water bottle from the fridge.

Next time.

Right. His mom still thought that there would be a next time.

Call him crazy, but he was pretty sure that wasn't going to happen. Not when Bobby kept showing up every time he tried to confess his feelings for Isabel.

He was beginning to think that a relationship between the two of them that went beyond being friends was a fool's errand.

"Oh no." Sondra's voice cut through his thoughts.

He glanced over to her to see that she was wielding a spatula.

"Stop that," she said as she narrowed her eyes.

Jackson studied her. "Stop what?"

"That self-defeating look you have in your eye. The one that says you've given up."

Jackson furrowed his brow. "I haven't given up." Then he sighed as he shoved his hands through his hair. "I've taken steps to get closer to Isabel—she's the one that's been pulling away." He scrubbed his face with his hands. "It's just hard to keep going."

Sondra grabbed a plate from the stack next to the griddle

and began filling it with food. She handed it over to Jackson and pointed toward the table. "Your worries aren't something a good, hearty breakfast can't fix."

Jackson took the plate and made his way to the table. Sondra busied herself in the kitchen while he ate.

As much as he didn't want to admit it, his mother had been right. There wasn't much that her bacon, eggs, and waffles couldn't fix. By the time his plate was clean, he felt a lot better.

Leaning back in his chair, he rubbed his stomach and smiled over at his mom. Just as he was about to thank her, the doorbell rang. He furrowed his brow and turned in the direction of the front door.

"Well, now, who could that be?" Sondra asked as she set down the dish towel and made her way through the kitchen and out into the living room.

Jackson stood up from the table and grabbed his plate. It was probably just a package being delivered. He made his way around the counter and over to the sink, where he rinsed his plate before loading it into the dishwasher.

"He's right back here." Sondra's voice drifted back from the front of the house.

Confused, Jackson glanced up and almost dropped his plate. Isabel was walking through the kitchen, right toward him. She had a determined look in her eye as she approached.

"Isabel?" he asked, still not sure if he was seeing things.

Isabel nodded as she reached out and grabbed his arm.

"I need to talk to you," she said as she headed toward the back door, dragging him along with her.

Jackson didn't stop her. It wasn't until they were outside and the back door was shut that Isabel turned to study him with her hands on her hips.

"Did you hire a nursing service?" she asked. Her eyes were narrowed and there was an accusatory hint to her voice.

Not sure how to answer that, Jackson shoved his hands into his front pockets and shrugged. Finally, he sighed. "Yes."

Isabel's expression stilled as she studied him. Then she pinched her lips together and glanced around. Jackson could see the tears forming in her eyes.

"I'm sorry," he said as he stepped forward. He'd wanted to make her life easier, not make her upset.

Isabel closed her eyes as she shook her head. Then she sighed and glanced back over at him. "Did you pay for my car to be fixed?"

Jackson cleared his throat and then nodded slowly.

Isabel let out a laugh as she threw up her hands. She paced across the grass and then turned to stare at him. "Why?"

Jackson forced a laugh. Why was she here? So many questions were rolling around in his mind, but Isabel looked expectant, so he shrugged. "Because you're my friend."

And he knew that was all she could be to him. She was marrying Bobby, and that was that.

She narrowed her eyes. "I have lots of friends. None of whom were willing to spend hundreds or thousands of dollars on me." She took a step forward. "Why did you do it?"

Frustration coursed through Jackson as he dropped his gaze. Why was she doing this to him? It wasn't fair. She was spoken for. Why was she making him spill his feelings for her? Nothing could ever come of them.

"Isabel, I..." He held her gaze and then dropped his eyes to study the ground.

Suddenly, her shoes appeared in front of him. Startled, he glanced up to see her standing only inches away.

"Bobby is headed to Australia," she said, her voice low and hesitant.

Jackson furrowed his brow. "What? Why?"

She inched closer to him. "He's going to live his life, and I'm...going to live mine."

Jackson blinked a few times, trying to register what she'd said. Could it mean what he so desperately wanted it to?

"I'm not marrying Bobby."

Jackson felt frozen in place as he stared at Isabel. Did she really just say that?

Isabel inched even closer. "I don't love Bobby, and I was marrying him for all the wrong reasons." She peeked up at him through her eyelashes, holding his gaze.

"You don't?" he whispered, the emotions in his body taking over and choking his ability to speak.

She shook her head. "The person I love, I've loved for a very long time."

Jackson's heart pounded harder in his chest as he hoped he was interpreting her words correctly. "You have?"

She nodded. "But he broke my heart, and I'm scared he'll do it again."

Jackson winced. What she said was true, but it hurt when he thought about her in pain. "I'm sure he's sorry."

She paused before she glanced back up at him. "Why did he leave?" she asked.

Tired of speaking in the third person, Jackson dipped down to meet her gaze. "Because I was scared. I thought I wasn't good enough for you."

Isabel furrowed her brow. "Why would you think that?"

Jackson sighed as he pulled back. "I wanted to marry you, Isabel. I did. But when I asked your dad for permission, he said...no." Jackson winced, holding his breath as he waited to hear what she had to say.

When he glanced back at her, she looked mad. "He did what?"

"He said I wasn't good enough for you, and that he wouldn't bless our marriage." Jackson shoved his hands into his pockets as embarrassment crept up his neck. He hated saying these things to her, and he most certainly didn't want her to admit that they were true.

Isabel pinched her lips together as her expression turned contemplative. "I love my dad, but he can be an idiot sometimes." Isabel inched closer to Jackson and brought her fingers up to brush them against his arm.

Shots of electricity rushed across his skin from her touch.

"He can?" Jackson asked, as he found himself leaning into her. Everything about her, from the way she smelled to the way she felt next to him, was so familiar it made his whole soul ache.

Isabel nodded as she allowed him to thread his fingers through hers. "He had no right to say any of that to you. Not when I chose you." She peeked up at him. "You're my person, Jackson Braxton. You've always been my person. I may have tried to forget that after you left, but what's written on the heart is hard to erase."

Jackson reached up and cradled her cheeks, reveling in the feeling of her skin under his fingertips. "Your heart?"

She nodded, tipping her face toward the palm of his hand. "It belongs to you. Eight years didn't change anything."

Every part of her was beautiful to him, from her soft pink lips to the way her blonde hair was picked up and tossed by the breeze. She was made for him to love, that much he was sure of.

"But you have to promise me that, no matter what, you won't run again. Dad's not too lucid, and he may say or do mean things, but you have to know that's not how I feel." She brought up her hand and pressed it against Jackson's heart. His skin tingled from her touch. "You're in my heart no matter what."

Jackson took his free hand and wrapped it around her waist, pulling her toward him. His body warmed from the feeling of her pressed against him. It was like they were two puzzle pieces that were once lost. Always and forever made for each other.

He drew his lips closer to hers, eager to rediscover the love and passion he'd once found there. Isabel responded by tipping her face up and inviting him in.

He held back, wanting to utter those three little words. The sentiment that he hadn't been able to utter to anyone else. Not since he'd walked out of Honey Grove eight years ago.

Because those words uttered to anyone else would have been a lie.

"I love you," he whispered as he drank in her gaze.

Isabel's eyes glistened with tears as she nodded. "I love you."

Hearing those words coming from Isabel's lips was all Jackson ever needed. No amount of success would ever take the place of the pure love he felt from Isabel.

Not wanting to wait another second, Jackson dipped down and pressed his lips to hers.

Fireworks. Electricity. A roaring fire. None of those could describe the heat that exploded through Jackson as he lost himself in her. Her lips were familiar, yet new. Years had changed the two of them. They were mature. More able to love completely and wholly.

It took their kiss to a level that Jackson had never experienced.

Love, when given and received, is the most powerful thing in the world. Finally, Jackson realized what those Hallmark movies had been talking about. What his brothers were experiencing.

And he'd found it, once again, in Isabel.

Wanting to look into her eyes and get lost in her gaze, Jackson pulled away and rested his forehead against hers. His lips were tipped up into a permanent smile.

"Wow," Isabel whispered as she rested her hands on his chest and met his gaze. "Where were kisses like that when we were younger?"

Jackson chuckled as he cradled her cheek and ran his thumb over her lips. "I promise never to go anywhere. I'm yours. Forever."

Isabel studied him and then tipped her lips to his hand and planted a kiss on his palm. "I know."

Jackson wrapped his arms around her and pulled her to his chest. He finally had her back, and he was never going to let her go.

"So, things are fixed?" Sondra asked, appearing next to them.

Jackson pulled away and glanced down at Isabel, who smiled and nodded.

"Yes."

Sondra got a disgruntled look on her face.

Jackson shot her a confused look. "What's the matter, Ma? I thought this was what you wanted."

Sondra nodded. "It is. I just...well, I didn't get the chance to intervene like we talked about."

"Intervene?" Isabel asked, shooting Jackson an incredulous look.

Jackson chuckled as he pulled his mom into a hug. "She was going to play interference with Bobby while I pulled you to the side and confessed my love."

Isabel raised her eyebrows. "There was a plan?"

Sondra nodded as she pulled back from Jackson and wrapped her arms around Isabel. "Only because I already love you like a daughter. Ask any of my other children. I interfere when I love you."

Isabel laughed. A light, joyful sound. It filled Jackson's ears and made him feel like he was home.

"Well, Mrs. Braxton, I'm honored," Isabel said as she hugged Sondra back.

Sondra turned so she could wrap an arm around Jackson. "Since you were in such a hurry to marry Bobby, does that mean I hear more wedding bells in the future?"

Jackson shot his mom a knock-it-off look, but as he brought his gaze over to Isabel, he saw her smiling at him. Relief flooded his body as he realized that she felt the exact same as he did. He loved her and had no intention of ever letting her go.

But proposing to her right now, in front of his mom, wasn't the way he saw it going.

"I guess you'll just have to wait and find out," he said, dropping his arm from his mom and gathering up the woman he loved, dipping her as he pressed his lips to hers.

Through the cloud of complete joy he felt in holding the woman that would become his wife, he heard his mom laugh.

"Those are the kind of surprises I love," Sondra said.

Isabel pulled back and met Jackson's gaze. "Me, too," she whispered and then kissed him again.

EPILOGUE

JENNA

JENNA SAT at the head table, alone. She was leaning forward, her arm wrapped around her stomach. Loud music boomed from the speakers on either side of the dance floor. Family and friends were dancing around, laughing and having a good time.

Something that Jenna couldn't seem to make happen for herself.

Coming home to Honey Grove had seemed like a good idea. Especially when Jackson had agreed to be there for her. Now, he had his arms wrapped around Isabel Andrews, and he looked as if he had no intention of letting her go.

Jenna was happy for her brother, she really was. It was just that if he'd been around, there was a good chance she wouldn't have made the huge mistake of kissing Dean.

Her foster brother.

She groaned and grabbed her fork. After pushing the

food around on her plate, she stabbed a piece of chicken and slipped it into her mouth.

Only she would mess up this royally.

She cared about Dean, she did. But when it came to relationships, she stunk. Dragging her brother's best friend into her life was a mistake. She wasn't even sure she knew how to have a real relationship.

Realizing that she just wasn't hungry, Jenna set her fork down and leaned back in her chair.

Her gaze wandered over to Dean, who was sitting on the other end of the table with his arms crossed and his jaw set. He was staring—probably a bit too hard—at the dance floor.

Her trip to Honey Grove had been going so well. Because Jackson was MIA, she had found something in Dean she hadn't known existed. He'd been her friend when she needed him. And then she'd messed things up.

Realizing that Dean deserved some sort of explanation for her going radio silent, Jenna gathered her courage and stood from the table. All she had to do was tell Dean it had been a mistake. That she wanted to take back her stupid kiss.

Then things could return to normal.

The walk over to Dean felt like it took a lifetime. By the time she got there, her resolve had wavered. After all, she was never good at the whole "feelings" thing. Many stunted relationships were the proof of that. What if she messed this up, too?

She didn't want to lose Dean.

So she stood there, behind his chair, staring hard at the back of his head. Ways to start the conversation rolled around in her mind, but none of them seemed to work.

Just as she forced herself to step forward and speak, Dean shifted in his seat, moving to stand. Suddenly, he was inches from her face and looking quite startled.

"Jenna?" he asked, shifting back to look at her.

Embarrassment flooded her body as she stepped away from him. "Sorry. I didn't mean to startle you."

Dean held her gaze for a moment before he moved to lean against the table. Once he was settled, he folded his arms. "Are you okay?" he asked. His voice was deep, and she could hear the concern there.

Jenna swallowed as her throat suddenly went dry. "Yes." Then she stumbled to say, "No."

She winced as Dean's eyebrows rose.

Sighing, she gathered her courage and faced Dean. She could do this. She could. She was an adult, and Dean deserved to be treated with respect. "Listen, about the other night..." Her voice drifted off as the memory of Dean's lips on hers flooded her mind. Emotions coursed through her, and she was pretty sure her cheeks were as pink as the flower girl's dress.

Dean was studying her when she returned her gaze to him. She couldn't quite read his expression, and fear filled her mind. When had she become such a blubbering idiot?

Suddenly, Dean rested his hand on her arm. Warmth

from his fingertips rushed across her skin. She pulled back, as if his touch had burned her.

"I wasn't in my right mind. I'm sorry. I didn't mean to drag you into my crazy life." She kept her gaze on the ground in front of her, too afraid of what his expression said.

"Jenna, it's okay." Dean's voice was soft and understanding.

Jenna looked up to see his smile matched his tone. He had his hands in his pockets, and he was leaning forward to meet her gaze.

"I'm sorry," she whispered.

Dean shrugged. "Don't worry about it. It was a one-time thing, and if you want me to forget it, I will."

Jenna pinched her lips together as she nodded. "Thanks."

Dean's smile faltered for a moment before it came back in full force. He glanced around and then back to Jenna. "If that's what you need to move on, then I'll give it to you."

Jenna wrapped her arms around her waist and nodded. Even though her stomach was in knots, she knew herself. Every one of her relationships or attempted relationships ended in pain. And she was a fool to think things would be different with Dean.

"It is," she said.

Dean held her gaze for a moment longer before he nodded and excused himself. Jenna watched as he made his way over to the bar and ordered a drink.

Relief and sadness contrasted themselves inside of her stomach.

She was grateful that Dean was willing to move forward as if nothing had happened. It really was the right thing to do. After all, if she tried to have a relationship with Dean and it fell apart, what would happen then?

Whose side would her family choose? And would she even be able to ask them to do that?

No. Kissing Dean had been a mistake. One she was determined to never make again.

It should be easy to do. After Jonathan and Tiffany's wedding, she was headed back home. Away from Dean.

And away from the feelings that lingered inside her heart.

**

Read Dean and Jenna's Romance in the Braxton Brother's Series

Christmas in Honey Grove

HERE

Jenna is home for Christmas and she's just trying to survive her mom's insistence that she get married, and her feelings for Dean that haven't really disappeared. Showing up with her new fling seems like the best way of avoiding both of them.

Dean can't seem to move on past Jenna. Even though all the people he knows and loves want to see him married, he can't help but hope that he and Jenna made a mistake. That perhaps, she feels the same way.

He didn't expect her to show up with a guy on her arm.

Both Jenna and Dean are determined to move on from the kiss that haunts them both. If they tried harder, maybe their hearts wouldn't hurt like they do.

Christmas time is a magical time, but does it hold enough power to mend their broken hearts?

Grab Your Copy
HERE

Missed the first Braxton Family Romance?
Josh and Beth's story
Coming Home to Honey Grove
HERE

Join my Newsletter!
Find great deals on my books and other sweet romance!
Get, Fighting Love for the Cowboy FREE
just for signing up!
Grab it HERE!

She's an IRS auditor desperate to prove herself.
He's a cowboy trying to hold onto his ranch.
Love was not on the agenda.

Made in the USA
Las Vegas, NV
07 March 2023

68719881R00132